MADELEINE TAKES COMMAND

Madeleine Takes Command

by

Ethel C. Brill

Illustrated
by

Bruce Adams

BETHLEHEM BOOKS • IGNATIUS PRESS
WARSAW, N. D.   SAN FRANCISCO

Originally published by Whittlesey House, 1946

Foreword and special features
© 1996 Bethlehem Books
All Rights Reserved

ISBN 1-883937-17-5
Library of Congress: 96-83472

Cover art by Bruce Adams
Cover design by Davin Carlson

Bethlehem Books • Ignatius Press
R.R. 1 Box 137-A, Minto, ND 58261

Printed in the United States of America

Acknowledgment

I wish to express to Miss Jeanette Eaton my appreciation of the interest she has taken in this story and of her valuable criticisms and suggestions.

Most sincerely,

ETHEL C. BRILL

Contents

Illustrations

Foreword

THIS NOVEL'S historical setting, based firmly on fact, compels our admiration for the bravery, honor and quick wit of the early French Canadians, and for one young woman in particular. Madeleine de Verchères, at 14, is the oldest daughter of a titled family living in "New France" in 1692. The Verchères wear moccasins and live in a log fort, but despite this frontier setting their pride and sense of honor stem from the French civilization they have brought with them, including its commission to plant Christianity in the New World. Madeleine's remarkable ability to "take command" shows a character shaped by the standards and wisdom of the Old World, vigorously tempered by the challenges and dangers of the New. This blending of the best of two worlds is demonstrated in Madeleine's own grasp of the situation at hand and in the way she manages to win the respect of the entire seigneury: young and old, men and women, soldiers and *habitants.*

Ethel C. Brill wrote this story in 1946—before the time when writing about either Native Americans or "old-fashioned" feminine virtues became so ticklish a business. The conflict between the French and the Iroquois, which forms the core of the plot, could be told in all its simplicity; Madeleine could be shown as a courageous female who had no time to lament that she was not a man. Yet, by dealing conscientiously with her material, Mrs. Brill, even in the face of today's politicized movements, powerfully and accurately captures a moment in history for the modern reader. *Madeleine Takes Command* is a stirring tale of suspense and fortitude, and a fine exemplar of a young girl's wisdom.

Early in the story we learn that the Iroquois killed the oldest of the Verchères sons. Now his younger brother Louis exclaims, "I would like to kill every single one of those vile Iroquois!"

Madeleine tempers this hot mood: "Hush, Louis! They are ignorant and wicked, but they are God's creatures. And through God's grace—I pray that they may be saved!" She goes on to remonstrate: "Do you think the white man has always been kind or even just to the red man?" They discuss a previous governor's cruel and unwise policies. "Anyone can see why [the Indians] hate us and want their revenge." Louis still thinks the Indians deserve to perish. "Even the Christian Indians?" Louis is asked. But in his eyes, "those mission Indians are the worst."

This little verbal conflict, between the voices of reason and hasty judgement, in the persons of sister and brother, provides the framework for the events that fill the remainder of the story. We can never forget the distinctions Madeleine has made. And in the book's epilogue we learn that mission Indians in historical fact did play an important role in rescuing settlers whom the raiding Mohawks, in the course of events, had captured.

In the midst of a suspenseful trial of nerves with the Indians, Madeleine simultaneously exercises her reason and her charm on another front, that of her own family. She brings to bear her ideals, her womanly ways and good sense upon her younger brothers. And they respond. Under the force of extreme pressures Madeleine proves that authority and a tender family intimacy need not exclude each other. This likable girl, often at the end of her wits and bone-weary, shows us all how that combination is achieved. The touchy, argumentative Louis honors his older sister in the end with a gallant gesture. She has brought out the best in all those around her, even her younger brothers. Her life and her courage, revealed against an exciting historical background, have yet much to say to young people of today.

Statue of Madeleine de Verchères
from a photograph, Canadian Railway Systems

I

Left to Hold the Fort

ALTHOUGH IT HAD been fifteen minutes since Madame de Verchères had put on her bonnet and fur cape, she found excuses to linger in the big living room of the manor house on the St. Lawrence River. Now she changed the position of a candlestick. Now she shifted a log in the blazing fireplace. Once she tried the bolt on the heavy door, and once she straightened a stack of snowshoes in a corner of the room.

Gravely her fourteen-year-old daughter followed these movements. Madeleine understood perfectly why her mother could not make up her mind to go. At last she came over and put a hand on the woman's arm.

"*Maman*," she said in a low tone, "you cannot pretend any longer that there is a single thing to do here."

"I hesitate to leave, Madeleine. If I had not promised your father, I would not go one step."

"Of course you must go, *Maman*. You will not be away long, and we shall be quite safe, the boys and I."

1

"I wish I could be sure of that. The business must be attended to, and I may not have another opportunity to make the journey. But I cannot help feeling that it might be better to take all of you with me."

"The canoes will be crowded, *Maman*. And I couldn't go to Montreal like this." Madeleine glanced down at her Indian moccasins and a skirt of coarse homespun woolen no better than that worn by the poorest girls in New France. "There is no time now to make ready. And who would command here? Is there anyone we could trust? No, Mother dear, the boys and I must stay."

Madame de Verchères put both arms around her daughter and held her close. "You are brave, my Madeleine. We must be brave in this dangerous country of New France."

"It is our own country, *Maman*," the girl said softly. "Don't be anxious about us. I will take good care of the boys."

"I know well that I can trust you, my daughter, but you must be careful and discreet as well as brave. I have told the boys they are to obey you in everything, as they would your father or me. Keep them close. Do not let them wander in the woods. Alexandre will make you no trouble, I think, but Louis is more reckless. You must be firm with him. Where are the little ones?"

As she spoke, a door was thrown open and a chorus of childish voices cried, "Hurry, *Maman*, the seigneur is waiting."

Madame de Verchères smiled down at her three youngest children—two small girls in bonnets and cloaks and a boy of five obviously very proud of his blue hooded coat, a miniature of the capote worn by Canadian soldiers. Then she raised her eyes to a shaggy, weather-beaten figure behind them, a man in homespun and buckskin who bowed low before her.

"Pardon, Madame," he said in a low apologetic voice, "but the seigneur bids me ask you to make haste. We must leave at once or night will overtake us."

"Indeed, yes, I will be with you in a moment. You may take my portmanteau."

He shouldered a worn leather bag that had been brought from France many years ago. Madame de Verchères gave a quick glance around the big room. Then, linking her arm through that of her daughter, she followed him into the open.

It was on an October afternoon in 1692 that mother and daughter stepped out of this home which, though built of roughhewn logs, was nevertheless known as a manor house. It belonged to an estate that King Louis XIV of France had granted to Sieur François Jarret de Verchères, the father of Madeleine, in return for his military services. Like other estates on the upper St. Lawrence, it was known as a military seigneury. And, like his neighbors, Madeleine's father was called a seigneur.

This estate of eighteen square miles was more than a home. It was a fort thrown up against the Iroquois nation. Those five tribes of Indians, headed by the ferocious Mohawks, were forever invading Montreal and the country around it. Therefore, when Madame de Verchères and her daughter left the manor house, they were not in the open. They were in an enclosure known as the stockade.

A gate that was always bolted at sunset led from the stockade to the banks of the St. Lawrence. Careless of the stumps and stones that roughened the ground, the three younger children of Madame de Verchères ran along up to this gate and soon they were lost from view. Their mother, however, picked her way. It was not until she had passed through the gate that she lifted her eyes. She could see the St. Lawrence flowing swift and mighty about the sharp point of land on which the seigneury was built.

"Look, Madeleine, look!" she cried, stopping short and pointing to the river. "Ah, is it not beautiful, *chérie,* our land of New France?"

"Yes, *Maman,*" returned the girl solemnly. "I always feel that, no matter how hard our life is, our country is worth it all."

As soon as they passed through the gate, they could look down on the dock at the edge of the river. Two canoes rested beside it, and on the shore directly in front of it a group had gathered to watch them depart.

A tall elderly man separated himself from the group and scrambled up the bank of the river. Although he wore buckskin breeches and moccasins over his hose of home-knit wool, his faded coat was of fine material and good cut. Plainly here was not one of the lesser folk clustered about the dock. Here was a seigneur.

He raised a broad-brimmed hat of beaver felt. "I am honored, Madame de Verchères," he said, "to have the privilege of escorting you today."

"You are kind, Monsieur. My business in Montreal is urgent or I would not trespass on your kindness. I am sorry if I have kept you waiting."

"Not at all, Madame. Mademoiselle Madeleine is to accompany you?"

"If only she could!" sighed the mother. "But, as you know, she is the eldest of my children at home and she must take charge of the seigneury."

The seigneur made a deep bow to Madeleine. "So Mademoiselle holds the fort. How I regret that I cannot have the pleasure of serving under such a charming commandant!"

Madeleine's cheeks reddened. Except for a few months now and then in the convent school of the Ursuline nuns in Quebec and for rare visits to the fur-trading and mission center, Montreal, she had spent her fourteen years in the isolated seigneury. She was little used to courtly speeches.

"I fear I am a very inexperienced one, Monsieur," she replied.

"Do you think there is any real danger now?" the mother inquired.

"I trust not, Madame. So far as I know, there are no signs of trouble at present. But here on the upper river we must be on the alert always. You have a garrison?"

"His Excellency the Governor has given us a few men of the militia and has supplied us with ammunition enough to withstand any ordinary attack."

"Then I think you have no cause for fear."

They were nearing the group by the river's edge when two boys scrambled up the bank and ran toward them. The taller, who was about twelve, wore a leather hunting shirt over his breeches. His younger brother wore the blue blouse of a peasant. Although their brown legs were bare, moccasins protected their feet.

"Oh, Mother," cried the elder, "can't we go too? There is room in the canoes."

"No, Louis, you must stay here and help Madeleine take care of the seigneury."

The boy's face fell, and he kicked at a pebble with his moccasined toe. "There's not a bit of danger here now," he muttered. "The sergeant says so."

"My boy, here in New France there's always danger," put in the seigneur a little severely. "You wouldn't desert the garrison, would you?"

Louis glanced up at him and stopped kicking at the stone. "I didn't mean to desert," he protested. "I meant, couldn't we all go?"

His mother laid a hand on his shoulder. "Not this time, my son. If your father were here, it would be different. Don't you remember what he always said—that one cannot put too much trust in strange soldiers? That's why there must always be some member of the family left in charge. So—be good, Louis. Obey your sister just as you would your father or me. Remember you must uphold the honor of the Verchères."

While she spoke, the seigneur had been staring impatiently in the direction of the canoes. "Madame," said he, "I do not like to press you, but the hour grows late."

"Yes, yes, Monsieur." She drew Louis, then Alexandre, to her and kissed them. "The good God keep you, my brave sons."

As the five figures advanced, the crowd that had almost obscured the boats parted. With yelps of delight the three youngest children, Jean, Angélique, and Cathèrine, who had reached the dock many minutes before, welcomed their mother. Then, after hurriedly embracing their sister and the two boys, they began besieging the seigneur with questions. How long would it take to get to Montreal? In which canoe was each to sit?

Smilingly the gentleman placed Madame de Verchères and the small boy on the folded blanket in the center of the first canoe. To Angélique and Cathèrine he gave the place of honor in his own canoe. The four oarsmen assigned to each craft raised their paddles.

"En avant!" cried the leader. The paddles dipped and the party was off.

It was a primitive mode of travel for the lady of the

The paddles dipped and

the party was off.

manor, but neither she nor her children thought about that. There was no other way of going to Montreal. Even the Governor of the colony traveled by bark canoe. No road connected Quebec, the capital, with the only other real towns, Three Rivers and Montreal. The St. Lawrence was the highway. Unless the traveler followed the river, by boat in summer or on the ice in winter, he had to make his way on foot over Indian trails. Practically all the population lived along the banks of the great river and its tributaries.

Twenty miles was not a very long journey. But to Madeleine and the two boys, as they stood watching the canoes driven against the current by the muscular arms of the canoemen, the undertaking seemed a truly serious one. If the times had been peaceful, they would have felt no anxiety about their mother's trip. But the times were not peaceful. For eight years and more the folk along the St. Lawrence above Three Rivers had lived in almost constant dread of the Iroquois. The country above Three Rivers had to bear the brunt of Indian wars. The settlements around Montreal and for nearly a hundred miles below could be reached easily by the fierce warriors, who came from their own country by way of Lake Champlain and the Richelieu River. Raiding parties appeared suddenly, now in one place, now in another, to kill, burn, and destroy wherever they could take by surprise the seigneuries, the tiny villages, the isolated farms, and even the forts.

Madeleine had faith in the courage of the neighboring seigneur and his men. She was glad that her mother had the opportunity to travel with him, but for all that, she was anxious and would be until the business in Montreal was finished and the home trip safely over.

The tenant farmers—habitants, as they were called—waved and cried good luck before they went their various ways. Soon Madeleine and her brothers were the only people left on the shore. Soberly they watched the two frail boats racing upstream. Silently they went back to the stockade. As they passed in, ten-year-old Alexandre asked, "Shall we close the gate?"

"Of course not," Louis answered. "Whoever heard of closing the gate until everyone is in from the fields?"

Madeleine replied more gently, "No, Sandre, we will wait until sunset as usual."

Leaving her brothers to their own devices, she re-entered the manor house and went through to the kitchen. There she was surprised to find one of the guards gossiping with Nanette, the one maidservant of the family. All but two of the squad of militia were out patrolling around the field where the habitants were at work. In those dangerous days it was not thought safe for the people of the seigneury to scatter to their various farms. All worked together in one field and then went on to another, and always with an armed guard.

In the spring of that year 1692, raiding bands of Iroquois had kept the country around Montreal and for many miles down river in continual alarm. Seeding had been delayed, the fields farthest from the stockade had lain untilled, and harvest was late in those that had been planted. Though the middle of October was now past, there was still work to be done, fall plowing and clearing and burning of refuse, before winter settled down on the St. Lawrence. So the soldiers had gone to the fields with the workers, leaving only two on guard within the stockade.

As Madeleine came through the door, the man who had been talking with Nanette turned around a little sheepishly. He was one of the ten guards sent by the Governor to protect the seigneury.

"So, Gatchet? You can find nothing to watch but Nanette cleaning fish?" Madeleine tried to make her tone as gentle as possible.

"La Bonté is in the bastion by the gate, Mademoiselle," returned the man sulkily.

"But how about the rear bastions? A man certainly ought to be stationed on one of those, too. If only so many of you did not have to be out in the fields guarding the workers, I should keep four men in the stockade."

As she met his eyes, almost insolent in their amusement, her cheeks flushed. "No, Gatchet, I am not just a frightened girl. But I know what happened here at this very seigneury two years ago, and I tell you it can happen again."

"The sergeant has given us no such orders, Mademoiselle."

"Very well. I shall talk to the sergeant himself this very evening."

Without another word the guard turned on his heel and walked out of the kitchen. Madeleine stared after him, and as she did so, she wondered anxiously about the next few days. If Indians should attack them, how far could she trust men like this?

II

Madeleine Assumes Command

"FISH AGAIN!" grumbled Alexandre as he came into the kitchen about an hour after Madeleine's conversation with the guard. He stared contemptuously at the fish cooking on a spit in the big fireplace.

"And what do you expect, my young lord?" jeered his brother, who had followed him from the stockade. "Perhaps venison. Ah, you would have been a fine one indeed to have been along with Father when he first came to New France. How about those times when the supplies gave out and the men didn't have a bite to eat?"

"Come, boys, don't waste words. We haven't much

14

time left to dress for dinner," said Madeleine, from her seat by the kitchen table.

"Oh, dear, do we have to dress tonight—even when Father and Mother aren't here?" Looking down at the hunting jacket that he loved, Louis groaned. "If you knew how often I wished I were Jacques Brunet and could stay in the same clothes all day!"

Madeleine lifted her head. "Jacques Brunet is a very nice boy. But he is the son of an habitant—not the son of the Sieur de Verchères. Just because we are living here in a wild new country, we must not forget the ways of Old France. Now run along, both of you."

"Well, you'd better run along yourself," Louis said, staring from her moccasined feet to her rough garments. "The daughter of the Sieur de Verchères looks not one whit better than the daughter of an habitant." With that he turned on his heel and started for the stairway leading to the bedrooms.

Alexandre followed him, but halfway up the stairs he ran back to poke his head through the door. "Do we get the preserve of wild plums with honey?" he called.

Smilingly Madeleine nodded.

"Good!" he cried. "That will make up for those everlasting fish."

When they had gone, the girl began to set the big table in the kitchen. Though they were poor and the house in which they lived was built of logs roughly squared with an ax and very unlike the great stone manor houses of France, the family of Verchères were gentlefolk. They would have scorned to lower the standard of their table service, however simple the food. As Madeleine spread the worn and carefully mended linen cloth, she sang softly a chanson, which, like silver, glass, and linen, had come from old France.

> *"Isabeau s'y promene*
> *Le long de son jardin,*
> *Le long de son jardin,*
> *Sur le bord de l'ile.*
> *Le long de son jardin*
> *Sur le bord de l'eau,*
> *Sur le bord du vaisseau."*

> "Isabeau was walking
> Up and down her garden,
> Up and down her garden,
> On the shore of the island.
> Up and down her garden
> At the edge of the water,
> Just beside the shipping."

As she finished the first stanza, she heard a voice from the big room. "Ah, Ma'm'selle, how charming that sounds!"

She turned to see an old man of eighty enter the kitchen. Although his military coat was shabby, it was clean, and nothing could have been neater than the

*She turned to see an old man of eighty
enter the kitchen.*

white hair that he wore in a queue tied with an eel-skin.

"I'm afraid you're too kind a critic, Laviolette," she returned with an affectionate smile. "The dear sisters in the convent at Quebec do not think so highly of my voice."

"Nonsense, nonsense. You sing like a young bird, fresh and strong and happy just because you are alive. When I hear you, I forget that I have ever seen an Indian or a wooden fort or a stockade. I am back once more in the beautiful France."

"Ah, dear Laviolette, I'm sorry you ever had to leave it." As she spoke, Madeleine placed on the table a loaf of dark wheaten bread that she herself had made.

"No, Ma'm'selle, do not say that. For then I should not have had the honor of serving under your father in the finest of regiments. And today I should not be here watching over his children and—"

"Mademoiselle," interrupted Nanette, turning the fish on the spit, "excuse me, but you must hurry to dress or the fish will be burned to a crisp."

"Yes, Nanette. It won't take me more than a minute." With a wave of her hand to the old retainer she hurried up the stairway.

When she came down, the two boys were waiting for her. As she gave an approving glance at their scrubbed faces, their clean linen, and their cloth coats, they in turn measured the transformation in her. This evening she wore over her velvet dress a jacket of crimson silk fastened with a gold brooch. Buckled shoes had replaced the moccasins.

"I like that jacket Father bought you in Quebec," remarked Louis.

"I do, too," piped up Alexandre. "Only—oh, how I wish he'd buy me a new coat! I'm sick of this old purple thing. Look at the sleeves—they're inches too short."

"I don't care anything about a coat if he'd only come back himself," said Louis. "I wonder—do you suppose, Madeleine, that Governor de Frontenac will ever release Father from military service so he can stay home with us?"

"I don't know, Louis. But don't you suppose that most of our habitant boys and girls are wondering the same thing about their fathers? Of course, your friend Jacques Brunet is lucky that his father, being the blacksmith, can't be spared."

It was a really handsome table to which the three young people sat down. The candles that lighted it were in silver candlesticks, though the meal consisted merely of a platter of fish from the river, a dish of mashed turnips, a loaf of dark wheaten bread made from the coarse flour ground in the seigneurial mill, with butter the girl had churned herself, and a little of the preserve of wild plums sweetened with honey, of which the boys were very fond. A spoon and a clumsy two-tined fork of heavy silver were laid at each place. As was the general custom, the boys used the knives they carried in leather sheaths at their belts, and their sister had her own smaller sheath knife.

They talked of many things, these three young people who spoke the French language and inherited the traditions of a titled French family. Were their mother and the three youngest children nearing Montreal by this time? Too bad the seeding had been so long delayed that spring because of Indian attacks. What a lot there was to do before winter. And to think there was only one young man on the place who hadn't been drafted for military service. Antoine alone was left.

At the mention of the young habitant's name Louis looked up from his platter. "Listen, Madeleine. Did Mother speak to Antoine about those missing pickets before she left?"

"What missing pickets, Louis?"

Louis banged his knife down upon the table. "Oh, why don't you and Mother listen to the men about this place? I've been talking for a whole week about that gap in our stockade. With all those bushes so near it—bah, what could be easier for the Indians than to slip through there?"

"But I haven't heard a word about it. I swear to you I haven't."

"Well, then, hear about it now. That hole must be filled in at once. Since I first told Mother about it, two more pickets have fallen."

"Then let's have Antoine set them up tomorrow. What could be easier?"

"It's not a question of setting them up, Madeleine. They're rotted. Yes, and so are a lot more of our pickets. We've got to have new stakes."

"But this is terrible, Louis. I can't understand why Mother ever let such a serious thing go."

"Mother didn't," interposed Alexandre. "I heard her only yesterday begging Antoine to fill in that hole."

"And why won't he do it?"

"His sweetheart, Madeleine," grinned her younger brother. "That's why he won't do it."

"His sweetheart? What do you mean, Sandre?"

"Just what I say. He's engaged to a girl at St. Blain and every night he sneaks out to see her."

"Oh, so that's it." Louis slapped his thigh. "He creeps through the hole in the stockade. Of course, if he went out through the gate, somebody would tell on him."

Madeleine's face grew stern. "So? He would risk this whole seigneury for the sake of his sweetheart. Wait till I see him. Perhaps I can catch him in the stockade tonight."

"Not tonight or any other night, Madeleine," said Alexandre. "Oh, last night I wish you could have seen him. I went out to look for my drum and fife when whom should I see but Antoine with the hood of his blue capote drawn over his face and the gayest red sash you ever saw. He looked like a cock. I tell you there's not a happier man in all New France than he is. Just think of his luck—hurting his leg so he couldn't go to fight the Iroquois."

"I call it infernal luck," Louis exclaimed. "Not to get a chance at those savages! Oh, just wait till I'm two years older."

"What are you going to do?" questioned Alexandre. "Slay them all with your own hands—Mohawks, Senecas, Oneidas—all the rest of the five tribes?"

"I would if I could! I would like to kill every single one of those vile Iroquois!"

"Hush, Louis," remonstrated his sister. "They are ignorant and wicked, but they are God's creatures. And through God's grace—I pray that they may be saved!" Bowing her head, she crossed herself.

"God's creatures!" exclaimed Louis passionately. "The fiends who killed François!"

At the mention of the sixteen-year-old brother who had been killed the year before in a campaign against the Iroquois, Madeleine looked solemnly into the fire. No wonder her mother had hated so to leave. After the death of this beloved son, parting from any of her family meant just one thing—the Iroquois.

Many moments had gone before she could speak. "François—yes, and many another brave Frenchman, too, has been killed by them. Yet let us be honest, my brothers. Do you think the white man has always been kind or even just to the red man?"

"They had no reason to complain of Governor de Frontenac's treatment of them," returned Louis.

"Ah, but after he went back to France, what then?"

"Yes," admitted Louis, "I suppose Governor de la Barre's campaign was a mistake."

"A mistake!" piped up Alexandre. "Father always says that it started all our worst trouble with the Iroquois."

"Exactly so," said Madeleine. "And what did we accomplish by the campaign only five years ago? Burning down their villages, chasing them from place to place. Anyone can see why they hate us and want their revenge. Oh, that mission Indian was right when he told Father we had burned the wasps' nest and left the wasps themselves."

Louis set his teeth. "I don't care what you say. The Iroquois are a cruel treacherous breed. They deserve to perish—every one of 'em."

"Even the Christian Iroquois, Louis?" asked his younger brother.

"Pouf! Don't talk to me about those mission Indians. They're worst of all when they turn."

Madeleine stared into the fire again. "You say they're cruel and treacherous. Come, Louis, have you forgotten what the Intendant at Fort Frontenac did to those Iroquois warriors he invited to a feast?"

"Took them captive and sent them to France for galley slaves," prompted Alexandre. "Yes, and it was a foul deed—one to make every true Frenchman blush."

"Well, defend them all you like," returned Louis. "But just wait, Sandre, till you see them again, crawling like snakes through some gap in our pickets. Wait

till you hear their war whoops and see their toma-
hawks raised to—"

"Hush, hush, Louis!" cried Madeleine, stopping her
ears and springing up from the table. "I cannot sit
here and listen to you any longer. Come, let's make the
rounds before it grows darker."

While Nanette was clearing the supper table, Madeleine, with Louis, went the rounds of the stockade. Every
evening some member of the family made such a tour
of inspection to see that all the habitants were in and
that the gate was securely fastened. The workers had
returned from the fields, and the palisaded enclosure
was humming with activity. Log pickets twelve feet
high made this enclosure. They enfolded not only the
manor house but all its adjacent buildings—storehouses, a blacksmith shop, a chapel, and many little
cabins. At each corner of this quadrangle of walls was
a bastion, a two-story log structure that served both as
lookout and little fort. But the main stronghold against
the Indians was the blockhouse, two-storied and log-
built like the bastions, connected with the stockade
by a roofed passage-way. In times of danger this shel-
tered all the people on the seigneury.

Madeleine sought out the sergeant and asked him
to keep at least two of his men awake and on guard all
night.

"One man is surely enough," he protested. "You
forget, Ma'm'selle, that I have but ten, and eight have
been on duty in the fields all day. We must have some

time to sleep. If there was danger near, more guards would be needed, but all is quiet. There are no Iroquois anywhere in the neighborhood. They are less bold when they know that the forts are garrisoned and patrol parties are scouting the woods. And anyway, it is late in the year for them to strike at the settlements, now that harvest is over and winter is at hand."

"But they attacked La Chesnaye in November, and you know what happened there."

"True, Ma'm'selle, but that was three years ago when everything was so bad. Our great Governor, the Count de Frontenac, had been back in New France only a few weeks then. Now, with patrols out everywhere and the leaves falling from the trees, it would be difficult indeed for the savages to hide their movements. No, Ma'm'selle, they have returned to their own country long before this. We have little need to fear attack until the spring comes again."

"That may be," Madeleine replied, somewhat reassured by his confidence, "but we cannot afford to grow careless. How suddenly they came two years ago! We barely had time to take refuge in the blockhouse. It was only the goodness of God that prevented the whole place from being burned. They set fire to the palisades, and rain put out the fire. Then the Marquis de Crissasy came to our rescue. As long as I live, I shall never forget what a terrible time that was."

"Truly, Ma'm'selle, I have heard that story and how

brave Madame your mother proved herself. Had she not been brave and cool, there would no doubt have been fire and massacre. Sleep peacefully, Ma'm'selle Madeleine. My men and I will keep watch. Since you wish it, I will station two on the bastions."

III

The Story of Father Dollier

MADELEINE WAS up early next morning, but when she went into the kitchen, she found the old soldier there before her.

"Good morning, Ma'm'selle," he said. "You and the little birds rise early."

"Not so early as you, Laviolette. Is the oven fire ready to light? This is baking day, you know."

"I have not forgotten, Ma'm'selle. The fire is not only laid but lighted."

"Good. I should have known you are always to be trusted."

The old man's memory was indeed remarkable.

Rarely did he forget or neglect any of his numerous small duties.

The firelight revealed the long heavy table and flickered on the shelves and cupboards lining the walls. Except the baking, all the cooking for the family was done in the great kitchen fireplace. An iron crane held chains with hooks for pots and kettles, and there were two spits for roasting meat.

Early rising was the custom at Verchères, and the boys were on hand before breakfast was ready.

"Madeleine," Louis announced, "I'm going out to help Jacques today."

"Where are they going to work?" Madeleine inquired doubtfully.

"On the Brunet place."

"Oh, that is too far away, Louis."

"It isn't far, Madeleine, and I promised Jacques yesterday that I would go."

"Then you will have to break your promise," declared Madeleine firmly. "You ought never to have made it. You know Mother told you to stay here."

"But Jacques and I are not going alone. You can't expect me to stay cooped up right here every minute till Mother comes back."

"You needn't stay inside the stockade all the time, of course. You can go to the near-by fields or along the river for a little way, but not into the woods. And I am sure Mother would not want you to go as far as the Brunet farm."

"But it seems so silly, Madeleine. There are no Iroquois around. The sergeant said so last night."

"He doesn't really know. We can't ever be sure."

"Well, suppose we can't," protested Louis. "The field work has to be done, and the others take the risk. Why make a coward of me? The seigneur's sons ought to set an example of courage, not shut themselves up in the fort like frightened babies."

The lad's argument was a good one, and Madeleine, brave and high-spirited herself, sympathized with him, but she knew that she must not weaken.

"The seigneur's sons," she said firmly, "have greater responsibilities than Jacques Brunet has. You are an officer, Louis, and you are on duty here. You have been ordered to stay on guard. I'm sure you are too good a soldier to disobey orders the very first thing."

"A woman's orders," the boy returned impatiently.

Madeleine's eyes flashed. "Louis de Verchères," she cried, "how dare you speak that way about your mother? Have you forgotten two years ago? Where should we be now if she had not given orders and we had not obeyed them? We should all be dead and scalped, or worse yet, prisoners in some Mohawk town. And can you blame her if she feels anxious about you, after losing François last year? He died doing his duty as a soldier of the King, and it may fall to you and Sandre to die that way, too, some day. But that is no reason for taking useless risks. You know that as well as I do."

Louis did know it, and he knew, too, that his mother

was neither timid nor unreasonable. When the seigneury had been attacked so suddenly, no officer of
the King could have taken command with more cool-
ness and efficiency. And how brave she had been a
year ago when the news came that François had been
killed fighting the Iroquois at La Prairie! Louis hung
his head.

"I know, Madeleine," he said huskily. "All right. I'll
obey orders."

"Of course you will." Madeleine smiled at him though
her eyes were moist. "This is baking day, and I'm going to make some of those barley cakes you like so
well."

So Louis and his younger brother stayed near the
palisades. All morning Madeleine was busy with
household tasks. She had no time for idleness until
the baking was in the oven. That oven, which stood
outside the house near the back door, was a homemade affair built of clay plastered thickly over arches
of bent willow. It had an iron door and rested on a
framework of squared logs with a roof over it to protect it from rain and snow. The first time a fire had
been made in it, the willow twigs had been burned
out and the clay hardened. It had been used ever
since Madeleine could remember and was good for
many more years.

The fire, which the old servant had lighted so early,
was inside the oven on the clay floor and was kept up
until the thick walls were thoroughly heated. Then Lav-

Nanette, using a long-handled shovel, put in the dark wheaten bread and the barley cakes.

iolette raked out the embers and ashes, and Nanette, using a long-handled shovel, put in the dark wheaten bread and the barley cakes. The door was closed and securely stopped to prevent any heat from escaping. Madeleine knew from experience just how long it took to bake well-done crusty loaves.

Before noon rain began to fall, driving the workers in from the fields. Though she knew the field work ought to be finished and the palisades repaired, Madeleine could not be sorry that for a few hours at least there would be no temptation for her brothers to stray.

They begged for an early supper so that they might have a longer time to listen to Laviolette's tales, and she agreed.

"What is it, Mademoiselle and Messieurs, that you want me to tell you tonight?" the old man asked when they were gathered in front of the great fireplace, Madeleine seated on a stool with her knitting, the boys on the hearthrug.

"About Father Dollier at Ste. Anne," the two lads replied together.

Madeleine looked into the ruddy fire. There she saw the stalwart priest who, as one of the chaplains of the Carignan regiment, had shared all the terrible hardships that her father and Laviolette had endured when they came from France to march into the land of the Iroquois. Father Dollier was now head of the Sulpitian Fathers in Montreal, and seldom did the Verchères family see him. Yet always the tales of his heroism, as presented by Laviolette, had thrilled Madeleine and her brothers. And when he did come to the seigneury—who else could have so comforted Madame de Verchères when François fell at La Prairie?

Suddenly the girl looked up into the old retainer's face. "Yes, Laviolette. Do tell the boys again tonight that story of Father Dollier coming to Ste. Anne and your staying with him."

"And why does Mademoiselle wish that particular story tonight?"

"Because—oh, it's such a wonderful example of brave people sticking to their posts!"

His wise old eyes scanned her shrewdly, and he nodded. She knew he agreed that the heroic story would be a good example to the boys. Then, tapping the coals from his pipe into the fireplace, he began.

A moment later his three listeners were transported back to the days when young ensigns like their father made their first campaign against the Indians. Each rough fort where men were posted was supposed to have a priest, and Father Dollier, tall, brave, and fond of a good joke, was the favorite among them all. Once, although ill, he volunteered to make his way through the snow to Fort Ste. Anne and minister to the soldiers left on guard there through the dreadful winter. Laviolette had volunteered to go with Father Dollier, and the way was full of perils. As he described the trip and the arrival at the fort, the old man grew so excited that he often had to pause to get his breath.

"At the fort," went on Laviolette, "we found that a pestilence had broken out. The Father set about his work at once. Until he had made his rounds of the sick, he would neither eat nor rest. But it wasn't the sickness alone we had to face. Starvation was added to it. No supplies came from Quebec, and all we had was a little moldy flour and salt pork. I guess they thought we could live on game and fish. But soon we were too weak to hunt.

"There were sixty men at Ste. Anne, and soon forty were ill. Father Dollier and our young surgeon worked day and night. Eleven men died, and the Father himself fell sick, but he would not give up. I think it was his courage alone that kept him and the rest of us alive till spring came at last."

Madeleine knew that not until several years of terrible campaigns were the military seigneuries started. Soldiers were persuaded to settle as habitants or landowners under their old officers, who were the seigneurs in command. The seigneur held himself in honor bound to keep the outposts against the enemy, to obey the Governor's call and to join any move against the foe. One of these young commanders was her own father, the Sieur de Verchères. He wanted to stay in New France and was ever ready to serve country and King. He was in the ill-fated campaign advised by Governor de la Barre, and Laviolette was about to plunge into an account of that struggle, when Madeleine put down her knitting and rose to her feet.

"Father says that campaign started all our worst trouble with the Iroquois," she said. "Come, boys, it's time for bed. Thank you, Laviolette, for your stories. You won't forget to cover the fire?

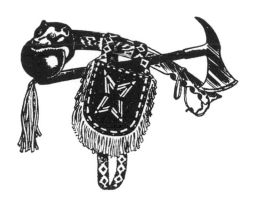

IV

Louis Deserts His Post

RAIN WAS STILL falling when Madeleine awoke. Her little chamber with its one window of small panes was dark. The whole house was cold and gloomy except the kitchen where the fire had already been uncovered. Nanette was beginning the breakfast preparations, and, as Madeleine joined her, old Laviolette came in with fresh water.

"A dreary morning, Ma'm'selle," he said, setting down the bucket.

"There will be little work done today, I fear," the girl replied. "Do you know, Laviolette, whether the new pickets are ready to be set up? Mother told Antoine to cut them."

"I have heard nothing of it, Ma'm'selle, but I will find out." He turned toward the door, but Madeleine stopped him.

"Don't go out into the rain again. You are wet now. Dry yourself at the fire or you will have trouble with rheumatism."

The old soldier smiled. "That is something that troubles me little, Ma'm'selle Madeleine. I am like old seasoned wood, too dry and tough to warp or crack." But he moved obediently to the fire and stood there drying his clothes.

The boys were late in getting up, and, since there was little for them to do, Madeleine did not disturb them. Breakfast was a less formal meal at Verchères than dinner or supper. Madeleine ate hers that morning with the two servants by the kitchen fire and later gave the boys theirs in the same place. Louis growled about the weather, for he hated to stay indoors. His sister quietly interrupted his grumblings with a practical suggestion.

"If you want something to do, you can set Antoine to repairing the palisades. It is not raining too hard for that."

Louis hastily swallowed his last mouthful of toasted barley cake. "All right. I'll order a *corvée*."

"You'll do nothing of the kind. You know Father never does that. All you need to do is to ask Antoine to get Brunet or someone to help him put in the new pickets."

"I was joking, Madeleine. I won't use the word *corvée*, never fear, though we have a right to demand their labor."

"Father has that right," Madeleine agreed, "but I'm not sure you or I have."

The privilege of *corvée* was the legal right of the seigneur to a limited amount of free labor from his tenants. In New France this privilege was generally used with moderation. The habitants were sometimes called upon for a few days' help in building manor house, church, mill, or fort, in making roads or clearing land, but the demands upon their time were seldom heavy or burdensome. At Verchères, in times of danger, the habitants voluntarily joined with the seigneur's family and his paid help in sowing and harvesting his fields, just as all worked together in turn on their own holdings. In old France, however, the right of the seigneur to unpaid labor was often used oppressively, and the peasants had come to hate the word *corvée*. Both Madeleine and Louis were well aware of that.

"Mending the palisades is for their defense as well as for ours," the girl said, "and it ought to have been attended to before."

Louis put on his blue woolen cap and opened the door. "A fine day for ducks," he remarked, and went away singing:

> *"Trois beaux canards s'en vont baignant,*
> *En roulant ma boule."*

"Three fine ducks came there to bathe,
Roll-ing my ball."

When he returned, in a very few minutes, he was not singing. "No *corvée* today," he said, pulling off his wet cap. "You can't mend palisades without stakes."

"Do you mean there aren't any?" Madeleine cried.

"Not here. Antoine says he started to cut some yesterday, but the rain stopped him."

"You tell Antoine," Madeleine said earnestly, "that just as soon as the weather clears, he must get those new pickets and set them up."

"I have told him. That gap is a bad one, Madeleine, and there are bushes so near that it would be easy enough for anyone to creep up there at night and slip in. If there were any Iroquois around, that would be the end of us."

Madeleine shivered. "The hole must be filled at once. It is almost a week since you boys found it." Suddenly she said in a firm tone, "Go and ask Antoine to come here to me. He must be more dutiful. I'm afraid he is thinking only of his sweetheart, and I cannot allow him to leave this place every night."

Louis hesitated, rubbing the back of his neck thoughtfully. "*Can* you stop him, Madeleine? Of course he has no right to open the gate. He doesn't do that. And we can block up the gap. But how can we prevent his climbing over the palisades if he wants to? He isn't a servant or a soldier. He's a free habitant, and I don't see how we can force him to stay inside if he wants to risk going out."

"It is a reckless thing to do."

"Oh, it isn't so dangerous, and Antoine is no coward. He can paddle along in the shadow of the shore and see or hear a canoe before anybody can see him."

"Just the same it is rash of him," Madeleine declared. "Mother would have found some way to stop him if she had known of it."

When Antoine arrived, Madeleine decided to receive him in the living room. She did not care to have Nanette or Laviolette listen to the interview. Antoine, the only one of the younger men remaining at the seigneury, was a good-looking fellow. Had it not been for his lame leg, the result of an accident when wood-cutting the winter before, Antoine also would have been in service.

Pulling off his woolen cap, the young habitant strode into the room. "I think I know what you want, Ma'm'selle," he said without a trace of embarrassment. "Those stakes, it is too bad I have not yet been able to repair them. But you know how belated we are this year with our work in the fields—how we've needed every man."

"Wait a moment, Antoine. Are you quite sure you don't find that gap very useful?"

He looked at her with startled eyes. Then suddenly those eyes began to dance. "Ah, so Ma'm'selle has heard that? We are to be married, Marie and I, when next the priest comes to St. Blain," he said with a smile that showed his even white teeth.

"You don't deny that you have slipped out at night?"

"Why should I, Ma'm'selle?"

"But this is too much, Antoine Giffard. Here you are actually smiling with pride when you've risked the whole seigneury for the sake of getting to see your sweetheart. Oh, Antoine, how could you?"

"That is not true," cried the young fellow. "I swear to you it is not true. Yes, I have used the gap to slip out at night, but how easily I could climb over the palisades! I am not deceiving you, Ma'm'selle. It is only because of the field work that I have put off the repairs. As soon as the rain stops, I promise you I will attend to it."

The delay worried Madeleine. She was relieved when, in the afternoon, the weather having cleared, Antoine and Brunet the blacksmith went to finish cutting the stakes. After the men had been gone over an hour, she happened to want Louis, and could not find him. Alexandre was sitting on a stump in the sun, just outside the gate, making arrows for his bow. When she asked him where Louis was, he shook his head. The last he had seen of his brother he was with Jacques at the Brunet cabin. How long ago was that? Sandre did not know exactly. Was it before the men went to the woods? Yes.

"Did Louis go with them?" Madeleine demanded.

"I don't know."

Madeleine hurried to the Brunet cabin. There was no one there. A party, accompanied by some of the soldiers, had gone to one of the fields. Only two soldiers, several old women, a few younger ones with little children, Laviolette, and Nanette were left within the stockade.

The anxious girl climbed the ladderlike stairway to one of the bastions, square log structures that over-topped and defended the four corners of the stockade. From the loopholes in the bastion walls, she had a good view of near-by fields, deserted except for hens scratching in the stubble and several pigs rooting about. Beyond the fields, where the ground rose higher, cattle and sheep were feeding in open pasture. But not a human being was to be seen. Strips of woodland, extending inland from the riverbank, hid the farther fields in which the habitants were working. Near the edge of the woods stood a log windmill, its big sails idle, for there was little wind. Those sails were homemade and crude in appearance, but all the machinery, except the mill-stones, had come from France, at no small expense to the seigneur.

"Were you here when Antoine Giffard and Brunet went to the woods?" Madeleine asked the guard stationed on the bastion.

"Yes, Ma'm'selle."

"Did you notice whether my brother Louis was with them?"

"I don't remember noticing him, Ma'm'selle, either with them or with the party that went to the fields."

Madeleine shook her head in perplexity. After an-other survey of the country round about, she descended from the bastion and crossed to the gate again. Alexandre was still there.

"Perhaps Louis and Jacques are out on the river," he suggested. "I'll go see."

She went with him to the riverbank. No one was in sight, and the small canoe the boys used lay bottom up in the shade of a clump of bushes. Nevertheless, Madeleine lingered, calling Louis again and again. There was a chance that the two boys had taken some other boat and that they were somewhere on the water, hidden by a bend in the shore, an overhanging bank, or an island. But if they were on the river, they were too far away to hear her.

"He must have gone with Antoine," Sandre concluded.

"I'm afraid so."

"They'll be back by sundown, Madeleine. And there aren't any Iroquois around now. There really isn't any danger, you know."

"I suppose not, but you boys promised *Maman* you would stay right here. Don't forget that, Sandre."

"I'm not forgetting. I don't believe Louis intended to break his promise. He wanted to be sure they got the stakes. He told Antoine that hole ought to be filled up tonight."

Sandre was probably right, Madeleine thought. It was foolish to worry, she told herself as she returned to the manor house. Louis ought to have asked permission. He had not asked because he was sure she would refuse. It was hard, she knew, for an active, high-spirited boy to be kept in such close bounds, especially when the others went back and forth to the fields and woods, in armed parties, to be sure, but without hindrance.

Just before sunset the field workers came in, but Louis and Jacques were not with them. Half an hour later, when Madeleine was in the kitchen with Nanette, Alexandre burst in.

"Antoine and Brunet are back," he cried, "but Louis is not with them."

Madeleine dropped the knife with which she was cutting cabbage for soup and ran out after the boy. She found Brunet and Antoine unloading the stakes from a homemade, two-wheeled cart, drawn by a shaggy-hoofed Norman work horse.

"Antoine," she cried, "where is Louis? Wasn't he with you?"

"Why, yes, Ma'm'selle, he was with us at first and helped to trim stakes, but he and Jacques tired of work, as boys will. Aren't they here?"

"No, they haven't come back. You ought not to have let them leave you."

"True, Ma'm'selle," Brunet agreed, "but we did not know when they went. We were busy, and they must have slipped away very quietly. We supposed they were somewhere near by. When we were ready to leave, we called, but they didn't answer. So we thought they had come home."

"They will be here soon," Antoine said unconcernedly. "No harm will come to them, Ma'm'selle. M'sieu Louis will be back for his supper, never fear."

Antoine's unconcern and the smile on Brunet's face betrayed to Madeleine that they thought her overfearful and anxious. Her pride was touched. There were no cowards in the Verchères family, she would have them know. With an effort she controlled herself and even forced a return smile as she replied, "Yes, hunger will bring them, I have no doubt."

Not trusting herself to say more, she turned away. Louis was all right, she tried to tell herself, but she would have a word to say to him when he came. He had broken his promise, and she felt herself responsible for his escapade. Had she not promised her mother that she would look after the boys?

V

Madeleine Is Anxious

IT WAS NOT STRANGE that Madeleine was anxious. Most of her fourteen years had been spent in ever-present danger. The seigneury lay in the exposed country. Continually threatened with danger, the people of Verchères had become used to it, and most of the time they thought little of it. Yet in the backs of their minds was always the dread of the swift, silent, cruel Iroquois.

At first Verchères escaped attack, though the seigneuries along the Richelieu suffered from raiding bands in spite of the three forts that had been built there. The settlements around Montreal were also attacked by parties of Iroquois that came down the Richelieu, landed before reaching the fort at Chambly, and made their way overland westward to the St.

Lawrence. Verchères lay about midway between Montreal and the mouth of the Richelieu. Even when all
seemed peaceful in the immediate neighborhood of
their own home, the children heard tale after tale of
massacre, capture, and burning only a few miles away.
From up or down the St. Lawrence or in the rear
through the woods between Verchères and the Richelieu, the seigneury might be reached easily enough
at any time.

Madeleine remembered all too clearly the year 1688
when she was ten and Louis eight. It had been a terrible
one. The Iroquois promised peace but quickly broke
their promises. They pillaged to the very outskirts of
Montreal. They ravaged the Richelieu seigneuries. They
threatened Fort Frontenac and Fort Chambly. They fell
upon the habitants in the fields, and many farms were
left untilled. The fur trade was interrupted, also. With
the Iroquois in control of the upper St. Lawrence and
the Ottawa, the western Indians did not dare to come
down to Montreal.

The depth of that winter brought respite to the suffering frontier, but with spring the enemy appeared
again. Still Verchères escaped attack, but in August
came fearful tidings from up the river. At night, in the
midst of a hailstorm, a large band of warriors had
landed at Lachine on the upper end of the Island of
Montreal. Falling upon the sleeping settlement, they
had murdered and burned. With the appalling news
came the warning that the band had not withdrawn

from the neighborhood. Divided into smaller parties, the Indians were raiding and destroying over a wide extent of country. The messenger, on his way down river, had barely escaped capture. Luckily he had glimpsed the enemy first, passing like shadows in the dim light of early dawn. Days of constant alarm followed, for the Iroquois pillaged over twenty miles of territory and carried away, it was said, more than one hundred captives.

In June of that year war had been declared between France and England. King James II had been driven from the English throne, but France supported the deposed Stuarts against William of Orange. The outbreak in Europe made matters still worse in New France. The Iroquois were friendly to the English of New York with whom they traded. The more northern and western Indians, the Algonquins, Hurons, Ottawas, were allies of the French. To their everlasting shame, both sides used their Indian friends against their white as well as against their Indian foes. Governors and military leaders were to blame for this cruel warfare, but it was the frontier settlers who suffered most from it.

To handle the desperate situation, the King sent the Count de Frontenac back as Governor. He did not arrive until October, but he threw himself into his task at once. He prepared to send expeditions against the English colonies. He strengthened the garrisons in the forts on the St. Lawrence and the Richelieu. He supplied the

seigneuries with arms and ammunition. He kept patrols on the move in the attempt to guard the settlements and to pursue raiding parties. Yet on a snowy day
in November, the Iroquois fell on the seigneury of La
Chesnaye on the northwest bank of the St. Lawrence
near Montreal, killed and burned, and took many captives.

That winter was one of want and famine. The fields
over half of Canada had lain untilled or unharvested.
At Verchères only the land near the stockade had been
planted. Scarcely enough was gathered to keep the
folk alive until spring.

With the opening of the leaf buds and the melting
of the ice the Iroquois came again. This time Verchères did not escape. While the seigneur was away
on military duty, a party of Indians appeared so suddenly that Madeleine's mother barely had time to
herd her children and the habitants into the blockhouse. Nearly all the able-bodied men were absent
with the seigneur. Nevertheless, led by the lady of the
manor, Verchères made a stubborn defense for two
days until troops came to the rescue.

The Governor's efforts began to bear fruit that year
of 1690. Early in the spring he sent a strong party to
the distant fur-trading post of Mackinac. On the way
they routed a large band of Iroquois and so opened
the route to the west. In August, for the first time in
several years, a great fleet of western Indians arrived
at Montreal to trade. Furs were about the only things

The Indian trade was very important to the welfare of the country.

Canada could send to France in exchange for the manufactured goods and supplies that were not produced in the new land. The Indian trade was very important to the welfare of the country, and its suspension had meant poverty and suffering.

Just as the situation seemed to be improving, came news that the English of New York and New England were planning a great land and water attack on New France. An outbreak of smallpox turned back the land expedition, and only a small party, most of them Indians, descended the Richelieu. The New England fleet, under Sir William Phipps, sailed down the St. Lawrence in October and laid siege to Quebec. With reinforcements, among them the seigneur of Verchères and some of his habitants, Governor de Frontenac had arrived at Quebec in time. The stronghold of New France did not fall, and Phipps and his fleet were compelled to sail home again.

The following winter was fully as hard as the preceding one. Again, owing to Indian raids, the harvest was scanty. The Governor could send out no expeditions against the Iroquois, for blankets, clothing, ammunition, and food were lacking. At Verchères such men as were left, and every boy old enough, searched the snowy woods for game. Traps and snares were set for rabbits, squirrels, and other small creatures, but the ammunition was so nearly exhausted that it was reserved for defense and for sure shots at large animals. Large game was rare since deer and moose were scarce that winter, and if there were any bears, they were sleeping in hollow trees or inaccessible dens deep in the forest.

Verchères, with three miles of river front and extending twice as far back into the country, contained about eighteen square miles of cleared land, forest, brush, and meadow. Seldom were the more remote woodlands visited. Men dared not wander too far from the stockade lest they encounter some hunting party of hostile Indians. Squirrels, which were plentiful, and fish caught through the ice helped to supplement the scanty stock of flour and vegetables. The seigneur had owned a small herd of cattle, and many of the habitants had kept a cow or two, pigs, and chickens, but the Indians, the spring before, had killed or driven away most of the livestock.

As soon as the spring of 1691 approached, Iroquois alarms began again. In April, a large band camped near the mouth of the Ottawa River and sent raiding parties prowling along both shores of the St. Lawrence. Again the habitants along the river were forced to neglect the sowing of their seed and to stay close to the fortifications. Again patrols took the field, difficult though it was to keep them in clothes and ammunition. Most of the food for the soldiers was supplied by the half-starved settlers. And before the approach of their pursuers, the Indians faded away into the woods and slipped up the streams. It was in May of that year that sixteen-year-old François de Verchères was killed at La Prairie.

In spite of difficulties, the soldiers scored some successes that spring, attacking and dispersing parties of warriors. In midsummer up the St. Lawrence came the glad tidings of the arrival at Quebec of a strong squadron of ships from France with troops and supplies. An expedition was promptly sent against the Iroquois camp at the Ottawa, and the warriors vanished from the neighborhood.

As soon as they were sure the Iroquois were gone, the habitants went back to their field work. But in August came another alarm. A war party of English, Dutch, and Iroquois had started from Albany for Montreal. The French, warned in time, met them at La Prairie and drove them back.

At Verchères the harvest was good that autumn in the fields that had been seeded, and it was gathered without disaster. The following winter was not quite so hard, and near its close a runner on snowshoes reached the seigneury with news that heartened everyone. Troops had surprised an Iroquois camp on the Ottawa not far from the place where the warriors had camped the year before and had killed or captured almost every one.

As early in the spring as possible, field work was begun, but in seedtime the Iroquois appeared at the head of Montreal Island. Several attacks were made on them before they were driven away. On the whole, however, the spring and summer of 1692 were not so bad as the preceding ones. The western Indians came down to Montreal to trade. The Governor was able to increase the militia patrols. The Iroquois found raiding less easy and more dangerous.

Verchères had escaped trouble during spring, summer, and early fall, and now, in October, there had been no alarm for some time. All the Iroquois seemed to have withdrawn to their own country, and rumors reached the seigneury that another great campaign would be undertaken against them during the coming winter or spring. With Governor de Frontenac leading, there was hope of real success, to be followed by a lasting peace. Nevertheless, no one could be sure that the danger was over for that year.

As Madeleine walked back to the house after questioning Antoine, she found herself reviewing the long terrible history of Indian raids. And with each searing memory, her anxiety about Louis and Jacques mounted sharply. Suddenly she decided that she must take action.

In the kitchen she found Laviolette engaged in sharpening the big carving knife. "A search party for the boys must be started at once," she said to him. "It will be dark soon. Will you bring the sergeant to me?"

As the old man rose to obey, the kitchen door opened. There stood Louis, wet and muddy.

"Here is something for supper," he said, holding out a string of small fish to Nanette.

With a sudden feeling of weakness, Madeleine leaned back against the table. For a moment she stared at Louis and Alexandre, who had followed his brother in. She hardly knew whether to laugh or cry.

"Louis, where have you been? I have been so worried."

Louis was trying to appear unconcerned. "It's nothing to make a fuss about, Madeleine. Jacques and I went with his father and Antoine to get the pickets."

"You broke your promise."

He looked uncomfortable but made no reply.

"You didn't even stay with them. You and Jacques have been away by yourselves," Madeleine went on sternly.

"Only up the creek a bit. We didn't mean to stay, but the fish were biting so well it was sunset before we realized. When we got back to the place where the men were cutting, they had gone. Do you want these for supper?" He held up the fish. "Or is it ready?"

"More than ready. Go and wash and change your clothes. You are covered with mud."

"What can I say to him?" the girl cried to Nanette and Laviolette when the two boys had left the room. In her perplexity, she had to appeal to someone, and Laviolette was sensible and experienced, Nanette full of common sense.

The old man replied for them both. "It is not a deadly offense, Ma'm'selle."

"No, but he must not do such a thing again. I promised *Maman* to keep the boys safe. What can I say to make an impression on him?"

"Say nothing tonight, Ma'm'selle Madeleine. Wait until morning when you have both had time to think. Then appeal to his honor as an officer and a gentleman. M'sieu Louis is heedless and rash like most boys, but he is his father's son."

VI

The Iroquois

SUPPER WAS an unusually silent meal. Expecting to receive a scolding, Louis was prepared to resent it. He was so surprised when his sister said nothing more about his escapade that he could find little to talk about. Madeleine did not feel like conversation, and, between the two, Alexandre was as uncomfortable as if he himself had been the culprit.

There was no storytelling that night. When Madeleine had finished helping Nanette with the dishes, she found her brothers seated demurely at a little table before the livingroom fire, playing draughts. They went to bed early, and she followed shortly.

Louis was late to breakfast next morning, and as soon as he finished eating, he seized his cap and made for the door. His sister called him back.

"Wait a moment, Louis." Seeing his defiant expression, she added quietly, "I'm not going to scold you, but I want to ask you a few questions. You can at least answer them."

With an uneasy glance at Nanette and Laviolette across the room, he threw down his cap. "All right," he said gruffly.

"When I was looking for you, I asked the soldier on guard if he had seen Antoine and Brunet start for the woods. He said he had, but you were not with them."

A grin banished the boy's sullen expression. "He couldn't see us. I told you about those bushes near the gap in the wall. Well, I said to Antoine that they ought to be cut down, but he didn't seem to think there was any danger of anyone using them for cover. So I made up my mind to show him how easy it would be. When he went out of the gate with the cart, Jacques and I slipped through the hole. You would scarcely believe it, Madeleine, but those bushes and sprouted stumps hid us so well that we reached the gully without Antoine or Brunet seeing us. Once in the gully it was easy to keep out of sight. You ought to have seen their faces when we bobbed up just as they started across the bridge. Of course the sentry couldn't see us either."

"But, Louis, that gap must be really dangerous!"

"It is. Antoine promised to cut down those bushes

this morning, and I'm—" Louis paused, then asked, "Did they put in the new pickets last night? I forgot all about it."

"I didn't," his sister retorted. "I sent Laviolette out after supper to see. He reported that by the time they had cleared away the old stakes and had dug out the broken, rotted ends, it was too dark to see to set up the new ones. Laviolette spoke to the sergeant, and he promised to post a sentry there."

"We'll get it done today," Louis exclaimed. "We must. It isn't safe." He picked up his cap and laid it down again. "You know, Madeleine," he said awkwardly, "I didn't mean to run away. I intended to come right back from the bridge. But the men thought we were going with them. Jacques' father told him to 'come along now and make yourself useful.' I couldn't turn back as if I were afraid."

"You had your fishing line."

"No, I didn't. Jacques had some twine, and I found a piece of fine wire in the cart. I think Antoine had used some to mend the harness. There didn't seem to be much we could do to help the men. So I suggested to Jacques that we try our luck. We made two hooks out of the wire and dug some worms. That was how it happened. I didn't mean to run away, truly. I won't do it again, I promise."

"You broke your promise, Louis," Madeleine told him sadly, "and deserted your post. Father would punish you, and so would Mother. You have made me break my word too, for I promised to keep you boys here. What are you going to do about it?"

This was not quite the sort of treatment Louis had expected. He was growing more and more uncomfortable, for he knew he was in the wrong. With sudden decision, he took the manly way out of the difficulty.

"I don't suppose there is anything I can do about it now," he admitted honestly. "I *did* desert my post. I'll punish myself, Madeleine. Until Mother comes back, I won't go one step outside the stockade without asking your leave. I'll keep my promise this time."

"All right, Louis. We'll say that you have given up your sword and put yourself under arrest."

Gravely Louis took his knife from the sheath and handed it to her. She received it with equal gravity. "I shall place it in the cupboard here," she said, "and Nanette and Laviolette will guard it until you have earned its return."

Louis raised his hand in salute, turned on his heel, picked up his cap, and marched out without another word. Smiling to herself, Madeleine went on with her work. She felt sure that he would keep his word this time.

In a few minutes he was back again. "I can't find Antoine anywhere. He must have gone to the fields. Old Jeanne says they made an early start. They want to get as much done as possible, for Brunet is sure that the weather will turn bad again before night. He is usually right about weather."

"But Antoine knew he was to put in those pickets the first thing."

Nanette had come into the room as Madeleine was speaking. "Is it Antoine Giffard you are asking for, Ma'm'selle? He has not come back from St. Blain."

"Not come back? Did he go there again last night?"

"Yes, Ma'm'selle, he goes nearly every night."

"I'll see if anyone is to be found," said Louis, and went out again.

Madeleine was angry. "Is Antoine in the habit of staying away all night?" she asked.

"Oh, no, Ma'm'selle. His mother says he has never done it before. She does not like these night trips of his."

"I should think not, indeed. Why hasn't Laviolette told me of this?"

"Perhaps he does not know it yet, Ma'm'selle. He—"

Nanette was interrupted by the appearance of the old man himself. He brought the same story but spoke in defense of the missing Antoine. "He is not in the habit of neglecting his work, Ma'm'selle. Doubtless he is on the way home now."

"I am going down to the river," Madeleine announced.

Laviolette followed her to the landing place. Out on the dock, Madeleine gazed upstream in the direction of St. Blain. No canoe was in sight.

The day had dawned bright, but the sky was clouding over now, and a raw wind, blowing against the current, ruffled the water. Some distance away was the island where their nearest neighbors, the Fontaine family, lived. But the Fontaines were all away now, and the fact increased the girl's feeling of loneliness. The afternoon before, when Madeleine had come down to the river to look for Louis, her mind had been so full of anxiety that she had had no eyes for the landscape. Now, as she glanced alongshore, she realized that autumn had advanced with startling speed. A few days had changed everything. When her mother had started for Montreal, the trees in the seigneurial forest had been rich with autumn crimson and gold. But the rainy weather had dulled their glory to ochre and brown and dark maroon. The leaves were falling fast, and many trees were already stripped. Under a cloudy sky, the island, which had been gay with color, had taken on a dull gray-brown varied by only an occasional fleck of brighter hue and the somber green of spruce and fir.

The old servant also was noticing the change. "It will soon be winter, Ma'm'selle."

"Yes. I hope Mother may have better weather than this for her return journey. We are going to have a storm, I think. I wish Antoine would come."

"He will surely be here soon. I would begin the work without him, but I doubt if I can handle those heavy pickets alone. I am tough for an old man, Ma'm'selle, but I haven't the strength in my muscles I used to have."

"You must not try it, Laviolette. Well, we can't bring Antoine by watching for him."

She left the dock but turned again at the top of the

bank for one more glance upstream. The old man paused, too.

"When do you expect Madame?" he asked.

"I don't know just when to look for her," Madeleine replied. "She hoped to finish her business in a day or two, but she may have to wait for an escort. I shall not really begin to expect her for three or four days yet. After that she may come any time, and when she is at home again, winter may close in as soon as it likes. Then for a few months we shall not have to worry about Ir—"

A musket shot cut short the word. As Madeleine swung around, there came another, then another. Were the guards firing to attract her attention, to call her back? No, they would not waste ammunition that way. Besides, the firing came from farther away, from beyond the stockade.

"Run, Ma'm'selle, run!"

At Laviolette's shout, Madeleine gave one startled glance at the nearest strip of woodland. Dark shapes were slipping out from among the trees. For an instant her feet were frozen to the ground.

"Run, Ma'm'selle!"

A musket roared. The shot went wide, though the foremost of those savage figures was scarcely a pistol shot away. The girl's momentary paralysis vanished. She flew over the ground with the speed of compelling fear. She did not follow the meandering path but took a direct course toward the gate, darting around stumps and bushes, leaping over logs, without being conscious of picking her way. Madeleine was agile, active, swift-footed. She could outrun both of her brothers and had often done so, much to their disgust. But swift though she was, she could not hope to outrun an Iroquois. They would gain on her. They were gaining on her. They would take her alive. Her only hope lay in the greater distance they had to go. If she could but reach the gate before they cut her off from it!

Another report. A bullet whistled past her head. "They think they may not catch me, so they are trying to kill me," she thought.

The way seemed to be lengthening out before her. Never had it been so far from the river to the gate. "Blessed Virgin, Mother Mary, save me," she prayed in her heart.

The unspoken prayer steadied her, seemed to give her strength for greater effort. There were more shots, and another bullet came by her ear, but she made herself turn to see if Laviolette was following. Yes, old man though he was, he had kept up with her. But where were the sentries? Why did they not return the fire? The cannon, too, which would have warned the other seigneuries and their own people—why could she not hear it?

"To arms, to arms!" she cried with all the breath she could muster.

If only they would make a sortie to her rescue! But the only reply to her shout was another shot from

"On, Ma'm'selle," he gasped.

behind her. Again she turned her head. Laviolette was still coming.

"On, Ma'm'selle," he gasped.

Eyes ahead, she darted forward. Two habitant women came running around the corner of the stockade. One was Jacques' mother. They reached the open gate just ahead of Madeleine. She paused, motioned them in first, looked around for Laviolette, then sprang through. A bullet barely missed the old man as he plunged in after her. Together they seized the heavy gate and swung it shut.

VII

Defense

AS SOON AS SHE had fastened the gate, Madeleine turned to the two women, who were crying convulsively. "Did you come from the fields?" she asked. "Are there others coming?"

"Ma'm'selle," the younger woman gasped, "I don't know. We didn't go out with the others. We had just started. We were only a little way beyond the fort when we heard the shots. Oh, Ma'm'selle, Ma'm'selle—my husband—I saw him fall."

"And my boy!" cried Jacques Brunet's mother. "The

67

fiends have seized my Jacques." She shuddered and choked.

Madeleine's heart was wrung with sympathy, but all she could say was, "Don't despair. Your menfolk may be rescued yet. Go to the blockhouse at once."

As the women turned away, Alexandre, white-faced through his tan, came running up.

"Sandre," Madeleine cried, "where is Louis? Where are our two guards?"

"On the bastions, aren't they? Louis sent me to look for you. He is guarding the gap."

"Good. Sandre, you go up to the bastion nearest the gate. Keep under cover, but if you see any of our people coming from the fields, let them in. Call one of the sentries to help you, and open and shut the gate as quickly as you can. Now, Laviolette—hurry—we must close the gap."

Laviolette, whose weary old legs had been seized with weakness and trembling as soon as they carried him through the gate, had dropped to the ground where he sat leaning against the pickets. He followed her to the spot where the pickets were missing. Here they found Louis, musket in hand.

"For Heaven's sake, where have you been, Madeleine?" cried the boy.

Madeleine saw that he did not realize she had been outside the stockade when the Indians attacked. Never mind. This was no time to tell him. "Come, Louis— quick," she directed. "Give us a hand with these." As

Here they found Louis, musket in hand.

she spoke, Madeleine tugged at one of the new pickets.

Laviolette laid hold of the other end of the fourteen-foot log, and Louis, putting down his musket, helped them to fit it into one of the freshly made holes. Feverishly they stamped on the earth they quickly filled in about it until at last it stood, stout and erect.

"One of them—thanks be to God!" panted Laviolette. "But those guards"—he looked from the north bastion to the one by the gate—"not a shot from them yet."

"And the cannon!" growled Louis, keeping one eye always on the thicket through which at any time some Indian scout might surprise them. "That should have been fired first thing. *Mon Dieu*, Madeleine, could it be true? Have the villains deserted us?"

Long before he spoke, the same fear had been gnawing at his sister. But she would give no sign of it. "Come—both of you—the second stake," she cried.

Feverishly they worked until all the stakes were planted. "There!" exclaimed the girl triumphantly as she surveyed the finished work. "Even if we haven't time for the cross timbers, these will stand up, no matter how hard a battering they get."

"Oh, they won't try to beat them down—not Indians," said Laviolette. "They'll wait their chance to slip through a weak spot or else climb over the wall. No, Ma'm'selle, direct attack is not their way."

"But we can't trust to that," said Madeleine. "If they

ever dream how small our garrison is—oh, there's no time to be lost. I must run to the blockhouse and prepare the ammunition."

"We'll go, too," said Louis, taking a step forward.

"No, no, you and Laviolette make the rounds of the wall. If there are any weak stakes, tighten them."

Without waiting for a reply, she hastened across the stockade. Alarmed by the first shots, most of the women and children had already taken refuge in the block-house. But as Madeleine passed one cabin door, she saw emerge from it a woman with a baby in her arms. Behind her a small boy and girl carried between them a heavy, homemade cradle.

Long before this dismal little procession reached the blockhouse, Madeleine was hastening through the narrow timber-roofed passageway that connected the stockade with this—the main fortress of every seigneury. Opening a stout door, she went straight to the section where arms and powder were kept.

The light was dim, for here there were no loopholes in the wall. Yet she realized instantly that there was someone in this room. It was a man crouching by one of the powder kegs, and as he turned around, the light from the door behind her fell full on his face. Her heart stopped beating.

"Gatchet!" she cried. "What are you doing?"

"I am going to blow the place up," he replied husk-ily. "It's better to die that way than by torture."

"You miserable coward," blazed the girl. "Take that

"Gatchet!" she cried. "What are you doing?"

thing out of here and stamp on it. Then go back to your post on the north bastion. Go!"

Her anger dominated him. Without a word he slunk away, the fuse shaking in his unsteady fingers. From a dark corner a second trembling figure emerged, his musket still in his hand.

"La Bonté, you, too! And no one on guard but Sandre! Do you know that while Louis and Laviolette and I have been working on the palisade, there has been only my little brother to guard the stockade? Run to your post and send M'sieu Sandre to me."

"I will go now—I promise you," the man stammered. "I will go straight back to the bastion near the gate."

Working with feverish haste, she selected muskets, pistols, powder, and bullets. The sight of a man's hat, an old one that had belonged to her father, lying on a powder cask, gave her an idea. She pulled off her linen cap and put on the hat. It was not too large over her heavy hair, and, seen above the pickets, it would deceive the Indians. She was adjusting powder horn and bullet pouch when Louis and Alexandre ran in with Laviolette at their heels.

"Arm yourselves quickly," Madeleine ordered.

"What is your plan, Ma'm'selle?" the old soldier inquired.

"To defend the seigneury to the last. The little children must stay in the blockhouse and their mothers with them. That leaves only six of us to guard the palisades. We must try to make the Mohawks believe that we have a strong garrison. If they attack, we can only do our best. We are fighting for our people—what there are left of them—for our country and our faith. Let us fight to the death if need be."

The two boys and the old man were standing very straight when Madeleine finished her brief speech. Louis' face was flushed, his eyes were shining, but little Alexandre was white. Following the old soldier's example, each raised a hand in salute. Then, in silence, they picked up powder horns, pouches, and weapons.

"Make the rounds," Madeleine ordered. "If you see any Mohawks within range, fire first from one loophole, then from another, to make them think we have plenty of men. Don't expose yourselves, but let the tip of a gun barrel be seen now and then. Call back and forth, shout orders, make plenty of noise."

The habitant women with their children had gathered on the upper floor of the blockhouse. As soon as she had assured herself that everyone was obeying her commands, Madeleine followed her brothers. In one of the bastions she found Gatchet and La Bonté and gave them their orders. They obeyed without question.

It seemed to Madeleine that hours must have passed since her flight from the river. She could scarcely understand why the Indians had not closed in. Through the loopholes in one of the rear bastions, she looked out on the near-by fields—part of the land reserved for the seigneur's own use—where the habitants had been working. She gasped as she caught sight of savage figures stooping over the fallen, and herding captives toward the woods. Swept by fierce anger, she raised her musket and fired. The man at whom she aimed, a tall warrior who was dragging away a boy of eight or ten, was out of range. Her shot was only a defiance, and the recoil of the heavy weapon almost knocked her off her feet. Although she was a good shot with a pistol, she was unaccustomed to a musket.

What she saw there in the field made her realize that the time since the first alarm had actually been short. She and Laviolette and Louis had been working in furious haste, while the Mohawks, in no hurry, had taken time to scalp and plunder, to pursue fugitives and to secure captives. They had let the stockade wait. Indians were always reluctant to attack a fortified post unless they could surprise it. Madeleine felt a quick sense of relief that the defenders, thank God, had reached their stations in time.

She wondered if other seigneuries along the river were being raided, and the thought recalled a duty not yet performed. Leaving the rear bastion, she ran to the one where the cannon was placed.

"La Bonté," she asked the man she had left there, "why have you not fired the cannon? We must warn the neighboring seigneuries and chance travelers as well."

"I will do it now," La Bonté replied.

"Yes, at once. We have heard no signals. If we are the first to be attacked, we must warn the others."

"And the men in the woods, too, Ma'm'selle. We do not know how far they have gone. They may not know what is happening."

"The men in the woods?" repeated Madeleine.

"Didn't you know, Ma'm'selle, that the sergeant and six men went hunting this morning?"

"La Bonté! Was no one guarding the workers?"

"Only two, Ma'm'selle, and they have both been killed, I think. You know, no one expected any trouble, and yesterday Gagnon found fresh deer tracks, so—"

Madeleine interrupted him. "Fire that cannon at once," she cried, "and frighten our attackers if you can."

This last news had almost unnerved her. The sergeant was overconfident, she knew, but she had not dreamed that he could be so careless and foolhardy as to take his men away on a hunt, leaving the field workers practically unprotected. It was no wonder they had been so completely surprised. She felt herself responsible, as if the fault had been her own, though she could not have foreseen such neglect of duty. The sergeant had been careful to say nothing to her or to her brothers about his intended hunting expedition. Was there no one she could trust? She was in command. She must see to everything herself, make sure every moment that everyone was doing his duty. A feeling of appalling loneliness swept over her.

VIII

The Sortie

THE BOOMING of the cannon roused Madeleine from her momentary disheartenment. If she weakened, what would become of her brothers and of the women and children in the blockhouse? The commander must keep up courage. She went on with her inspection of the defenses.

Madeleine decided to station one of her little army on each bastion, leaving the remaining two to patrol the palisades. When she reached the blockhouse, she found everything in confusion. The musket shots, the firing of the cannon, the shouts and whoops and yells, had convinced the women and children that the fort was being attacked. They were in a panic of fear, the crying and screaming of the more timorous affecting even the bravest.

To quiet the clamor was a difficult task. Not until she warned the women that the noise could be heard outside the fort and that it would encourage the Iroquois to attack, did they make any real effort to calm their little ones and themselves.

"You must be quiet," Madeleine said firmly, "and keep the babies quiet. Crying won't help a bit. It would be much better if you would laugh and sing. I know that will not be easy, but if we are to save ourselves, we must make those Mohawks believe we have such a strong garrison that we are not afraid of them. One of you must keep watch from each loophole. If you see any Indians coming near the blockhouse, call the guard in the nearest bastion, and he will protect you. I'm going to give all of you work to do."

Quickly, then, she set them to cleaning and loading all the muskets and pistols. Extra weapons, loaded and ready, were a necessary preparation for defense.

As soon as the women were calmed and set to work, Madeleine took up her own post on one of the bastions. La Bonté held the one with the cannon; Laviolette and Louis were on the others. Gatchet and Alexandre were patrolling the palisades. Sandre was a little fellow for such duty, but he was trustworthy. He would do his best.

The Indians were still busy plundering. They were driving away cattle and horses and catching the pigs that had been turned out to root and the chickens scratching in the harvested fields. Some were doubtless searching the woods for strays and fugitives. They held off from the fort, remaining, for the most part, beyond range. For a cannon they had the greatest respect and fear, and an occasional musket shot, now from one loophole, now from another, convinced them that an armed guard was keeping watch.

Determined to keep up the fiction of a strong force within the stockade, Madeleine shouted to La Bonté in as deep and husky a voice as she could manage. He roared a reply, and the others, who had fallen silent after their first efforts, took the hint and called back and forth as if repeating orders. How much of their noise could be heard at a distance they could not tell, but at least they hoped to deceive any Indian scout who might be creeping toward the walls. In spite of the seriousness of the situation, Madeleine could not help smiling at Louis' attempts to make his boyish voice sound like a man's and to vary its tones so that he might be mistaken for half a dozen men.

Time dragged on. Madeleine had no way of keeping count of the hours, for the one clock the seigneury possessed was in the manor house. Since the day was cloudy, she could not watch the progress of the sun. She had been on her bastion for a very long time, it seemed to her, when, looking toward the river, she saw a canoe between the shore and the nearest island. It was not Antoine's craft. Two people were paddling, one a little girl. There were other children, too, and a woman. They were not too far away for Madeleine to recognize their neighbor, Pierre Fontaine, his wife, and her three younger children.

At the moment Madeleine could not see an Indian, but she knew that, as soon as the enemy caught sight of the canoe, they would be on hand. No time could be lost—she must take action at once to save them. She called La Bonté from his post, hurried down to the gate, and summoned Gatchet.

"You must make a sortie," she told the two militiamen, "down to the landing to bring the Fontaine family to the fort."

Up to that moment the men had obeyed her unquestioningly, but this was too much.

"It would be madness," Gatchet protested. "We should be shot down in an instant, and no one would be left to protect you."

"We will support you by firing from the fort," she returned. "Will you go?"

"No, Ma'm'selle," the two answered together. La Bonté added, "Inside the fort we obey you, Ma'm'selle, but you have no authority to order us to go outside."

"Then I will go myself. Sandre," she called, "tell Laviolette to come and watch the gate. Get back to your post, La Bonté. Gatchet, take the other bastion. You will be safe there."

It was a desperate thing she was about to do, and she was very much afraid. But the thought of those children falling into the hands of the ruthless Indians drove her to desperation. She felt the greater responsibility for them because they were connections of her own. Their father had been André Jarret, Sieur de Beauregard, a kinsman of her father. After Jarret's death, the mother had married Pierre Fontaine.

Madeleine dropped her musket and opened the gate. With a backward glance to make sure that Laviolette was coming on the run, she hurried outside. Her heart was beating fast as she looked toward the river where the canoe was just drawing up to the landing. To right and left she glanced. There was not an Indian in sight. She started to run, then forced herself down to a brisk walk. If she went boldly, if she did not appear afraid, the Indians might think her going was a trick and hesitate to come near.

From the stockade came the beating of a drum. Who had thought to do that, to beat a drum as if the garrison were gathering for a sortie? She went on with more confidence, but with eyes straight ahead for fear of what she might see if she looked toward the woods. The way seemed very long, almost as long as when the Indians were chasing her. As she drew near the landing, the last of the Fontaine family, the girl with the paddle, had just stepped out of the boat.

"Hurry!" Madeleine cried. "The Mohawks are all around us! Let the canoe go."

Fontaine dropped the canoe that he had started to lift from the water and herded his frightened family before him. As Madeleine turned back, she forced down a gasp of fear. They had been observed. Painted figures were issuing from the woods. The war whoop chilled her blood.

In reply to the savage shout, the cannon boomed. La Bonté, though he had refused to go himself, was at least supporting her. Madame Fontaine and the children ran past her, but Fontaine waited for Madeleine to precede him. She waved him forward.

"Go on, but not too fast. Don't act as if you were afraid."

"Right, Ma'm'selle," he murmured with a nod. He spoke to his wife and children, and they obeyed him and slowed their pace.

The natural thing for the Indians to do was to cut the refugees off from the fort, but the warriors seemed to be in no haste. The cannon shot had made them pause. This was the time for the little procession to go forward boldly. It moved steadily on, first the older daughter, leading her little brother by the hand, then the younger, followed by the mother. A few paces behind them came Fontaine, his musket ready. Madeleine, pistol in hand, was last.

Within the stockade the drum was beating furiously; voices were shouting orders. It really sounded, Madeleine thought, as if the place were full of soldiers. As soon as La Bonté could reload, he fired the cannon again.

Deceived by the boldness of the girl's move, by the drum and shouts, checked by their dread of the cannon, the enemy hung back. Only a few came on, cautiously, taking care not to approach the palisades. One of them fired, and Fontaine swung on his heel and returned the shot.

The little party was drawing nearer the gate. To cut them off now the warriors must approach within easy musket range. And too close approach would certainly be the signal for a sortie if there were enough soldiers to make it.

So the Indians continued to hold back. They fired a shot or two, but they were not really eager to kill. They preferred to take the women and children alive. If they waited now and later found some way to surprise the fort, to enter and take it by strategy, they would get them.

Madeleine's whole life had been spent on the frontier. She knew these things. Indeed, she had counted on them when she made her rash venture. Her plan seemed to be succeeding, but she was desperately afraid. She wanted to run full speed for shelter and leave the Fontaine family to their fate. But she controlled herself, forcing herself to go at a moderate pace.

As they approached the gate, however, the refugees

could not resist the temptation to quicken their speed. Eleven-year-old Anne broke into a run, dragging her little brother after her.

The gate opened. Anne and the boy ran in. Fontaine, who had reloaded as he went, swung around and sent a shot toward the enemy. As he fired, the fort received his wife and little Marie. He and Madeleine darted through. And the gate closed behind them.

IX

Reinforcement

MADELEINE'S muscles went slack, and she leaned against the pickets. Then her eyes fell upon Alexandre, his drum hanging from its strap around his neck, his drumsticks in his hand, and the tears running down his cheeks.

"Sandre," she cried, "was it you who thought of that?"

He nodded and said chokily, "I wanted to go with you, but Laviolette wouldn't let me. Then I thought if I beat my drum, the Mohawks would think we were going to march out."

"You couldn't have done a better thing," Fontaine

exclaimed heartily. "You are a quick-witted boy. Some day you will be a general." He glanced around. "Where are your men, Mademoiselle Madeleine?"

"Dead in the fields and the woods. We have left only two soldiers, Laviolette here, my brothers, and myself. You are a most welcome reinforcement, Monsieur Fontaine."

He nodded gravely and glanced at his wife, white and trembling, and the children, big-eyed with fear.

"Take Madame and the little ones to the blockhouse," Madeleine replied to his thought. "The other women and children are there. The blockhouse is strong and well provisioned."

The mention of provisions made her realize that her little army must be fed. "Laviolette," she said, "I will take your bastion while you and Sandre get something to eat. Then bring me something. It does not matter what."

Laviolette saluted and turned away. Madeleine laid her hand on her little brother's shoulder. "Sandre," she said softly, "I think you saved my life. You are a brave boy and a clever one." She stooped and kissed him, then bade him go to his dinner.

Fontaine, Madeleine felt, would be a valuable addition to the garrison. He was brave, resolute, and dependable. While she was eating the bread and cheese Sandre brought her, the new recruit came to her bastion and put himself under her orders.

He told her that he and his family were on their

way home from Montreal. Traveling without escort, they had not seen or heard anything to alarm them until the booming of the cannon warned them of danger somewhere. "At first I thought of turning back and going up river to Boucherville," he said, "which is, as you know, well defended, but I decided that would take twice as long as to come on here. If you were surrounded, I hoped we might escape by crossing the river and following the shore on the other side of the islands. Everything seemed quiet. We came in sight of your fort and there were no Indians to be seen."

"No, they were in the woods and in the fields at our rear," Madeleine told him.

"So I turned this way," he went on, "intending to stop and ask what the warning signal meant. When we were near the landing, I caught sight of something moving at the edge of the woods. Then I saw you. Not until you called to us did I guess that the Mohawks were all around."

Fontaine agreed with Madeleine that the only chance of holding the fort until relief came lay in keeping the Indians convinced that the garrison was a strong one. "We can do nothing by force," he assented. "We are too few. Not our strength but our wits must save us."

"Yes, it is the only way," Madeleine agreed. "We have a fair supply of ammunition, and I have given orders to fire every time an Indian comes within range and to shout commands and make plenty of noise."

"God grant that the captives do not reveal our weakness!"

That such a thing might happen had not occurred to Madeleine. The thought troubled her, but she thrust it aside. "Not one of our people would betray us," she asserted stoutly.

Madeleine and Fontaine took the soldiers' posts, and Alexandre relieved Louis. When he had eaten, Louis came to his sister's bastion.

"Madeleine," he said, "why didn't you call me to go down to the river with you?"

"Because, Louis, it was a thing one person could do just as well as two. There was no need for both of us to expose ourselves. If I had been killed or captured, you would still have been here to take command."

"You might have sent me, then," he argued. "That sort of thing is a man's duty, not a woman's."

"So I thought when I asked Gatchet and La Bonté to go, and they refused," said Madeleine.

"The miserable cowards," Louis snorted. "I'm going to tell them what I think of them."

"No, no, Louis, you must not. We can't afford to anger them. They might desert or blow up the fort. We need them, and as long as I do not order them into too great danger, they obey me. We must not lose any of our garrison. As your superior officer, I forbid you to mention the matter."

"Very well, *mon capitaine.*" Louis saluted, but he added in a most unmilitary manner, "I suppose you are right, Madeleine, but the next time a sortie is made, I'm going to lead it."

"I think there will be no more sorties," Madeleine told him. "We mustn't risk our lives foolishly. Remember, whatever you do, don't try anything of the kind until you have consulted me."

"I won't if you will promise to do the same with me."

"I promise, Louis. You are my lieutenant. It is right that you should know my plans. No one is going outside the gate if it can possibly be helped. But you will have your full share of danger and responsibility, my brave brother."

"I want my share," Louis asserted sturdily.

Madeleine glanced through a loophole. All was quiet in that direction. Her eyes sought the squat tower of the mill showing above the trees. The mill, where the wheat and other grains raised in the seigneury were ground into coarse flour, stood on the bank of a stream that came down in rapids from higher ground. The building was a strong one of logs and heavy timbers and was loopholed for defense.

"I have been wondering," she said, "if any of our people have taken refuge in the mill. They could defend themselves there for a long time."

"If they had firearms," Louis added. "I haven't heard any firing from that direction, have you?"

"No. Oh, Louis, if this attack had come yesterday when—"

He interrupted her hastily. It was along that stream he had been fishing. "I know, Madeleine. I wonder where they will take Jacques and what they will do with him." He turned away, saying gruffly, "I must get back to my post."

The afternoon passed slowly. The thick clouds of the morning were broken and wind-blown now. Gusty blasts ruffled the river and whirled the ripened leaves from the trees. Patches of sunshine and shadow moved across forest and field. The fields and meadows in view from the fort, the rough clearing with its stumps and bushes, lay deserted. For long periods not an Indian was seen.

Then dark figures would appear, scarcely visible except when they moved, among the trees at the edge of the woodlands, or a painted, befeathered brave would slip across the open just out of musket range. Sometimes one or another of the guards discovered a sneaking scout, running, stooped low, from bush to bush, or crawling from behind a stump, trying to get near enough to the stockade to spy upon those within. A shot or two in his direction, to let him know that he was seen, caused him to disappear, to lie hidden, or to turn back. Each experience of this kind intensified the feeling that every bush and stump and inequality of ground might be sheltering a waiting, spying enemy. Even when all seemed peaceful, the threat of the Mohawks' unseen presence lay like a storm cloud over everything.

As time went on, Madeleine grew convinced that there would be no attack while daylight lasted, and the garrison showed itself on the alert. But how could the handful of defenders guard both the stockade and the blockhouse through the long hours of darkness? After puzzling over the problem for some time, Madeleine came to a decision. For herself and Louis her plan would be perilous indeed. He had a right to be consulted. She called Gatchet to her bastion and then went to her brother's.

"We must make our plans for the night, Louis," she said.

"It looks as if it might clear," he commented.

"Laviolette says there is a storm coming. Night is our most dangerous time. Of course, we can all go into the blockhouse and leave the rest of the fort to its fate."

"Not unless we have to," Louis protested. "If they find the palisades unprotected, they will ransack the place and set fire to the buildings. We have fooled them so far. It seems to me we ought to go on making them believe there are plenty of us to defend the whole fort. Don't you think so?"

"I do, Louis, but we can't leave the blockhouse unguarded. Someone we can depend upon must stay there tonight. Pierre Fontaine seems to me the best one for that duty. But one man can't watch all sides at once. I am thinking of putting La Bonté in there too. That will leave you and me and Laviolette and Gatchet on the bastions."

"How about Sandre?" asked Louis.

"He must go to the blockhouse."

"He won't like that," protested Louis. "He wants to do his share. Why not put him on the fourth bastion instead of Gatchet?"

"He is such a little fellow for so dangerous a post," said Madeleine softly.

"But he's no coward and Gatchet is," declared Louis. "We can't depend on either of those fellows. If you leave one of them alone on a bastion at night, he will get frightened and run for the nearest hiding place. Sandre may be little, but he won't desert his post, and he has quick eyes and ears, quicker than mine," Louis admitted generously.

Madeleine knew he was right. La Bonté and Gatchet were not dependable, and Sandre, child though he was, had already proved himself. "Go speak to him about it, Louis, but don't urge him," she said.

Laviolette's prophecy was fulfilled. The sun set red behind purple-edged clouds, and, soon after, the wind veered to the northeast, bringing more clouds. A fine, cold rain was falling when Madeleine, leaving Louis alone on guard, assembled the rest of her tiny army to give them their instructions for the night.

"God has saved us today from the hands of our enemies," she began. "Let us give Him thanks. Let us pray for the souls of those who have fallen, and ask Him to succor the poor captives."

She dropped to her knees on the wet ground, and the others, removing hats and caps, knelt opposite. For a few moments all prayed silently till Madeleine rose to her feet.

"Because God has been merciful to us," she said, "we must not grow careless. He expects us to do our part. The night is the most perilous time, and we must not fall into its snares. I want you to understand that I am not going to ask of you any duty that I am not ready to perform myself. For tonight, I, with my brothers and Laviolette, will take entire charge of the fort. You, Monsieur Fontaine, I put in command of the blockhouse. With La Bonté and Gatchet under you, you will guard the women and children. I do not need to tell you that the darkness and the storm will give the Mohawks the best of cover if they choose to attack. If the fort is attacked, you in the blockhouse must not attempt to come to our aid. Whatever happens to us out here, the blockhouse must not be taken. It can't be taken if you make any show of resistance. Do not surrender even if my brothers and I are cut to pieces and burned before your eyes."

Laviolette and Alexandre, eyes fixed on Madeleine's face, saluted. The two soldiers also raised their hands in salute but failed to meet their commander's eyes. They knew she did not trust them.

Only Pierre Fontaine protested. "Mademoiselle Madeleine, you have chosen the most dangerous duty for yourself. It would be more fitting to let these men," he pointed to the two militiamen, "guard the fort, under my command."

"No," Madeleine returned firmly. "In the absence of my father and mother, I am responsible for the seigneury and all within it. Louis comes next to me, and Alexandre has chosen to stay out here with us. We will stand watch and, if possible, keep the Indians believing that we are a real garrison. If we are actually attacked, if the enemy gets inside the palisades, we will retreat to the blockhouse if we can."

"If you can, Mademoiselle," Fontaine repeated significantly.

"If we can't, we will meet whatever fate God wills for us." The girl turned to La Bonté and Gatchet. "Go to your posts."

"To the blockhouse, Ma'm'selle?" Gatchet inquired.

"To the blockhouse, and obey Monsieur Fontaine's orders." When the two were out of hearing, she spoke hastily to Fontaine. "We cannot trust those men out here on the bastions at night. They might desert their posts at any moment. They did so this morning at the first alarm. In the blockhouse, under you, they can be of use. But keep an eye on them. Upon you and you alone I rely for the defense of those poor women and children. Your place is even more important and difficult than mine; so many lives depend on you."

"I understand, Mademoiselle," Fontaine replied, saluting now. "I will obey you as I would your father.

"I will obey you as I would your father, Mademoiselle,"
Fontaine replied.

But let me beg you not to be rash. If danger presses, retreat and join us before it is too late. Do not wait until the savages are within the palisades. Do not sacrifice your own life and your brothers' lives needlessly."

X

Night and Storm

MADELEINE WAS afraid of what the night might bring, terribly afraid. Death at the hands of the Mohawks, or captivity—could anything be worse than that? Yes, she told herself, to be a coward, to be untrue to her trust, would be worse. For her to seek safety in the blockhouse, to leave the fort to its fate before it had been actually attacked, would be to betray her trust, to betray her people, her home, her father and mother, her country. If the seigneury forts should fall, what would become of New France? Even the capture of one fort would increase the confidence and boldness of the enemy. They must hold Verchères if they could.

Two years before, when the place had been surrounded, Madame de Verchères had ordered Madeleine as well as her younger brothers and sisters into the blockhouse with the habitant women and children. But the mother herself had taken charge of the defense of the palisades. She had commanded a stronger garrison. Her force of armed men had been small but not so desperately inadequate as Madeleine's little squad. That made no difference, thought the girl. The duty of the Verchères was clear and must be performed to the end.

Madeleine wanted to spend a few minutes in the little log chapel praying for the delivery of the seigneury out of the hands of the enemy, praying for strength and courage for her brothers and herself. But with night approaching she dared not be away from her post longer. She went to her bastion, and there, looking out into the darkening dusk, into the gathering storm, she made her prayer.

The northeast wind rose to a gale, lashing the rain before it. The wind was bitterly cold, and the rain soon turned to sleet and icy pellets of snow that rattled against the timbers and swirled through the loopholes. It was a wild night indeed, just the sort of night when an Indian attack would surely succeed. In the darkness and the storm, not one of the sentries could see a yard beyond his bastion. How fatally easy it would be for the enemy to steal up in force and climb the pickets before a warning could be sounded! Even now they might be drawing near. Madeleine found herself shivering from head to foot, not so much with cold as with dread of what might be approaching, hidden in the stormy blackness.

This would not do. She must control herself. She must not let her imagination run on ahead to meet disaster. She remembered Fontaine's words, "Not our strength but our wits must save us." Wits must be kept working. The fort was too silent. There must be noise, plenty of noise. With the full force of her lungs, her voice as deep and heavy as she could make it, she shouted, "All is well!"

Laviolette echoed the words, then Louis, then Alexandre. The younger boy's voice had scarcely died away when Madeleine shouted a second time. Again the call went the rounds, and again and again, Fontaine and his men joining in from the blockhouse. How far their voices could be heard above the whistling of the wind, the hissing and rattling of sleet and frozen snow, Madeleine had no means of telling. She could not doubt that there were scouts lying under cover close to the walls. And those scouts must be deceived.

The shouting served the double purpose of keeping the sentries alert and of convincing the Mohawks that the defense was prepared and ready. Each guard had been supplied with several loaded muskets and pistols. The discharge of one weapon did not thus leave him defenseless while he reloaded. Now and then a shot was fired into the darkness, but Madeleine had given orders that ammunition was not to be wasted. No one was to fire unless he thought he saw something moving or had his suspicions aroused in some way.

It was very cold on the bastions in the wind and storm. Though she was wrapped in a heavy cloak, Madeleine had to keep moving most of the time to avoid being chilled through. If she stood still only a few minutes, her feet in their woolen hose and moccasins grew numb. From one loophole to another she passed, trying to see out into the blackness, and often getting a dash of stinging sleet in her face. A candle lantern gave her a little light at first, but when a gust blew it out, she did not attempt to relight it.

Slowly the night crept on, endless hours of darkness, storm, cold, and fear. She was not sleepy. Her anxiety was too great to allow her to grow drowsy, and the prompt responses to her cries of "All is well" assured her that all were on the alert. She had not been certain how it would be with the boys, who were not used to long watches.

It seemed to Madeleine that morning must be close at hand when she noticed that the storm was lessening. The wind had shifted and was not so violent. Snow was no longer falling. Though the sky was still overcast, her eyes, grown used to the night, could penetrate the darkness a little. Gazing through a loophole was not quite so useless and hopeless.

"Ma'm'selle"—it was Laviolette's old voice, hoarse and cracked from much shouting—"Ma'm'selle, I hear something. I cannot see it."

Madeleine strained eyes and ears but could make out nothing. Laviolette was on the bastion nearest the gate. With her cloak drawn close about her to keep out the sharp wind, she hastened through the darkness to join him.

"It is I, Laviolette," she announced, and moved swiftly to a loophole.

"Out there, Ma'm'selle. Do you see them?"

She did see them, bulky black forms against the snow-covered ground. They were moving slowly. But those black things did not look like human forms. She could hear the crunching of their steps in the icy snow, the sound the old man had heard before he could see them. That crunching was not made by moccasined feet but by hoofs.

"Cattle, Laviolette," Madeleine said with relief. "Some of our cows the Mohawks failed to catch."

"I think you are right, Ma'm'selle."

A plaintive moo came up from the creatures. It was followed by a shout from Louis. "*Qui vive?* What is happening there?"

"Some of the cows have come back." There was little danger that Mohawk scouts hearing could understand. They were unlikely to know any French though they might understand a few words of English or Dutch.

"Shall I let them in, Ma'm'selle?"

"God forbid!" A shudder of fear shook the girl. It had suddenly struck her as strange indeed that any of the cattle had escaped the raiders. "It may be a trick," she objected. "The Indians may be following, covered with the skins of the cows they have killed.

Perhaps they plan to slip in with the beasts when we open the gate. But we are not so simple as to be caught with any such device."

For some moments the old man and the girl stood silent, looking down on the dark forms moving about close to the gate and uttering pitiful moos from time to time.

At last Laviolette said, "Ma'm'selle, I do not think there are any Mohawks among those cattle."

"They look natural enough," she agreed, "but in the darkness we cannot be sure."

"It is not the way they look but the way they act, Ma'm'selle. Our French cows do not like Indians any more than they like wild beasts. The strange scent is enough to frighten them and make them take to their heels, but those animals—"

"Why, that is true, Laviolette," Madeleine interrupted. "Do you think we dare let them in? Their milk will be needed for the children."

"Ho, Madeleine," came Louis' voice again, "have you let in those cows?"

"Not yet," she shouted. "Is all quiet there?"

"All quiet." And Alexandre took up the cry, "All quiet!"

Madeleine cast another glance at the huddled cattle. She was now very sure that no Indians were among them.

But might they not be somewhere near, waiting their chance? They could not be very close to the gate, however. There was no cover there, no stumps or bushes close in. She could see no dark spots, except the cattle, on the snow.

"Louis! Sandre!" she shouted. "Come to me, at the gate!" Then to Laviolette she said in lower tones, "Keep close watch and fire down on anything that looks suspicious. Don't hesitate. It is much better to shoot a cow than to miss a Mohawk. I'm going to open the gate."

Louis and Alexandre reached the gate almost as quickly as she did. She gave them their orders. "Stand back a little, muskets cocked. As the cows come in, watch closely. If you see anything among them that might be a man, fire!"

Louis caught the idea at once. "You think the Indians may try to sneak in with the beasts? Stooped down beside them?"

"Or covered with hides. I believe everything is all right, but we must provide against surprise. Are you ready? Ready, Laviolette?"

Madeleine's hands trembled as she unfastened the gate. Perhaps she was doing a reckless thing, but the cows might be sorely needed for milk and even for meat before the siege was over.

As the gate began to swing open, the cattle crowded up. They pushed their way in eagerly. With feverish haste, the girl slammed the heavy gate and fastened it. Five cows, a mere remnant of the seigneury herd, were inside, and nothing but a blast of cold wind had entered with them.

Relieved though she was to have the cows, Madeleine quickly turned to her next task. The rest of the fort had remained unguarded too long. "Back to your posts, boys," she cried. "Never mind the cows. They will take care of themselves. Run! Shout when you get there."

Surely morning must be near at hand, she thought. As she was returning to her station, she noticed that the clouds had parted, revealing the stars.

She called back, "Laviolette, can you tell what time it is?"

His reply was slow in coming. To get a good view of the clear sky overhead he was obliged to go out on the ladderlike stairway that led to his post. At last he answered, "It is about two o'clock, Ma'm'selle, not later, I think."

Two o'clock! Hours yet until morning, hours of darkness and cold, of straining eyes and ears, of alarm at every sound and sign. One comfort Madeleine had. The night was not so dark now. Keeping watch for moving figures against the snow-covered ground was not so difficult, so impossible, as it had been in the blackness of the storm. But every dark spot of bush or stump was a menace. At any moment something might creep out from it. Time and again she thought she saw one of those black spots move and watched it, her heart in her mouth, only to conclude that her eyes had tricked her or the bush had been stirred by the wind.

She was not troubled with sleepiness, but she feared that one or another of the tired sentries might doze

at his post. At short intervals she started the cry of
"All is well." Of all the twenty-four hours, she knew
the period before dawn was the most dangerous. It
was a favorite time for Indian attacks. The Mohawks
had not taken advantage of the storm. If they were
going to make an attempt that night, it would be in
all probability just before daylight. The guards must
not be allowed to grow drowsy, and above all things
the enemy must not guess how few were holding the
fort.

With this thought in mind the weary little band
increased their shouts, their noise and clatter, as the
night wore on toward dawn. Sandre even made use of
the drum he had taken to his bastion, beating it furiously for some moments when the eastern sky began
to show signs of graying. "I thought," he explained
afterward, "if the Indians got the idea that we were
mustering to go out and attack their camp, they would
not dare come to attack us."

XI

A Long Day

DAWN CAME slowly while the anxious sentries watched and listened and shouted back and forth in ceaseless vigilance. Not until broad daylight did Madeleine feel sure there was to be no immediate attack. The night was over, and the fort had not fallen. The cry of "All is well" took on new meaning, and the girl breathed a heartfelt prayer of thanksgiving.

The clouds were broken and scattered. The east was flushed with the rose and pale gold of sunrise. But winter seemed to have come overnight. The ground was covered with snow, untracked save for the hoofprints of the cattle she had admitted. All appeared peaceful. Not an Indian was in sight. Fear and horror seemed like a bad dream. Was the nightmare over? Had the Mohawks slipped quietly away in the darkness? Madeleine might have believed so had it not been for wisps of smoke rising here and there among the trees. The enemy's cooking fires were alight.

Hearing the approach of steps, Madeleine turned from the loophole. It was Fontaine. "Good morning, Mademoiselle. God be thanked that you are safe and sound."

"And you also, Monsieur. How is everything in the blockhouse?"

"As well as could be expected. It was a night of fright truly for those poor women and children, fright and grief for the loss of their loved ones. But with the morning they are taking heart and courage. At present Marguerite and our little ones are sleeping. You must be very weary, Mademoiselle. Let me relieve you while you rest and take food."

"I prefer to stay here," Madeleine told him, "but if you will take Laviolette's place, I will send him to bring food for all. The boys must be starving."

"Very well, Mademoiselle."

"Tell Laviolette to eat something and to warm himself if he can. I fear there is not a fire burning. Bid him bring me whatever he finds without delaying to cook anything."

Though she had been awake all night, Madeleine was not conscious as yet of being very tired. Neither did she feel especially hungry. The cold barley cakes

Laviolette brought she ate mechanically, her thoughts on the problems and plans of defense. After she had finished and the old man had resumed his post, she made her way to the blockhouse to see for herself how things were there.

As she walked across the palisaded enclosure, she noticed how strange and deserted everything looked—the snow almost undisturbed, the manor house with its steep roof and great chimneys, the workshops and storehouses, the habitants' cabins, empty of life. Would the Indians notice that no smoke rose from the fort? Would they notice and wonder?

Madeleine found the women in the blockhouse recovered from the panic of the day before. They were self-controlled and steady now, going calmly about their makeshift housekeeping and caring for their children. For the sake of the little ones, they were even cheerful. They might give way to terror for a little while, but once the first shock and horror of the Indian raid was over, the habitant women had plenty of courage. Their bravery was an encouragement to Madeleine. If these women, with hearts full of grief for dear ones killed or captured, could be so brave, surely she, who as yet had lost no one, should not weaken.

They smiled at her as she came among them, and she felt that she did not need to worry about the behavior of the women—except one. Born and bred in Paris, Marguerite Fontaine had never grown used to the perils of the frontier. She was timid by nature,

Madeleine found the women recovered from their panic and caring for their children.

and this wild country had frightened her from the first. Madeleine found her weeping and clinging to her husband, who stood at one of the loopholes, musket in hand.

When the girl spoke to her, Marguerite let go of her husband's arm and turned. "Oh," she sobbed, "what will become of us?"

"Why," Madeleine returned cheerfully, "we shall come through all right. The night was the worst time and that is over."

"There is another night coming," Madame Fontaine persisted, shuddering. "Let us leave this place and flee to one of the King's forts where we can be safe."

"But," cried Madeleine, aghast at the suggestion, "we should all be killed on the way."

"Not if we go secretly after dark. We can cross the river and keep to the other side."

"We couldn't even reach the river. The Mohawks would discover us. There are too many of us."

"Then," Madame Fontaine declared, "if all cannot go, at least my husband can take the children and me. Oh, Pierre," she pleaded, "take us away at once. We shall be safer out there on the river than shut up here with savages all around us. Take us to Sorel."

Fontaine turned a worried face to Madeleine. Putting his free arm around his wife, he tried to reason with her. "I can't do that, Marguerite," he explained. "The risk would be too great. You don't understand. If Mademoiselle Madeleine should decide that this place cannot be defended and that we must try to retreat to Sorel, then we will all go together." He looked at Madeleine questioningly.

Madeleine slowly shook her head. "You must do as you think best. I shall not try to keep you here. But my brothers and I will not abandon Verchères. We would rather die than give it up to the Mohawks. You know as well as I do that they must not be allowed to take French forts. The fall of even one seigneury fort would be a disaster to New France. If they take one, they will think they can take others. They are afraid now to try to storm defended palisades. But if they succeed once, no place would be safe from there."

She spoke so warmly that Madame Fontaine ceased weeping and stared at her with wide-open eyes. The other women within hearing nodded, looked at one another, and murmured, "That is so." "Truly she is right."

Pierre Fontaine nodded also and said gravely, "You are quite right, Mademoiselle, and I, for one, will not desert you." Then to his wife, "Say no more, Marguerite. Even if I thought we could reach Sorel, and I don't think so, we are not going to try. As long as Mademoiselle Madeleine stays, we stay also."

"Thank you," Madeleine returned quietly. "Take heart, Madame. You and your children will be far safer here than on the way to Sorel. We have only to keep up our courage and hold the fort for a little while until help comes."

"How long do you think that will be?" the trembling woman asked fearfully.

"A day or two at the most. I should not be surprised if we were rescued before another night. Help may be near even now." Madeleine turned to Fontaine again. "Everyone must have some sleep today, for we shall all need to be awake again tonight. There are seven of us to do sentry duty. Four must be on the bastions all the time. Here in the blockhouse these brave women can keep watch during the day. If you, Monsieur, and one of the soldiers will relieve Laviolette and Alexandre for a time, they, our oldest and our youngest, can rest first. Louis and I will keep our posts."

"Very well, Mademoiselle, we are under your orders."

"There is another thing," Madeleine went on. "Fires should be made in the manor house and some of the cabins. If no smoke rises from our chimneys, the enemy will notice it."

"True," Fontaine agreed, "I had not thought of that."

With a lighter heart, Madeleine returned to her post. Madame Fontaine excepted, all in the beleaguered fort were behaving well. They seemed to be trying to do their best. Even La Bonté and Gatchet were doing better than she had expected. With God's help, the fort would hold out until rescue came.

The sky cleared rapidly. Though the wind remained cold, the bright sun was melting the unseasonable snow and ice. The premature winter was disappearing. It was autumn again. Sentry duty was not now such a chilling task, and Madeleine was soon able to discard her heavy cloak.

Unless by some ruse the Indians could get close to the palisades without being seen, she doubted if they would try a daylight attack as long as they believed the fort well garrisoned. She saw to it that the shouting and the noise were kept up. As on the day before, the approach of an Indian from any direction was the signal for a shot. There were few attempts to approach, however—few, at least, that the sentries discovered. How many Mohawks there might be within actual musket range, but hidden behind stumps and bushes, no one could tell. Perhaps there were none, perhaps a score.

Alexandre, old Laviolette, and Gatchet were the first to go off duty. Sandre left his post staggering with fatigue. Later, he returned yawning and stretching and admitted that he could have slept hours longer.

When Madeleine's turn came, she decided that, before settling down to rest, she would go to the blockhouse again and warn the women to keep close watch. As soon as the girl appeared, Madame Fontaine seized upon her and between tears and lamentations begged her to reconsider leaving the fort under cover of night. Their mother's agitation set the younger children to crying, and other little ones joined in.

Madeleine finally succeeded in quieting the clamor.

She did not try to argue with Madame Fontaine but turned her attention to the habitant women's questions. There were problems of their makeshift housekeeping to be solved, and disputes were referred to their young mistress for settlement. She examined the supplies and gave out to each family enough to last through the next breakfast. There was a fireplace in the blockhouse where cooking could be done, but not all could use it at once. Madeleine was called on to decide how the turns should be taken.

She bade the women bring from their cabins as quickly as possible the necessary bedding, cooking utensils, and other things left behind in their hasty flight. It might be safe enough for the families to remain in their own cabins during the day and to return to the blockhouse at night. But Madeleine dared take no such chance. The defenders were too few. If the Indians should storm the palisades by day or should manage to slip in somewhere, the women and children would have no time to reach safety.

At this point Nanette stepped forward. "Ma'm'selle," she said, "am I not a member of the seigneur's household?"

"Certainly, Nanette. Why do you ask that?"

"Because I have been kept in the blockhouse," said Nanette. "Why can I not serve as Laviolette does?"

"But you were needed here, Nanette. What would you do outside?" asked Madeleine, curious to know what was in her mind.

"Let me go back to the manor house this morning. There I can bake for all of us, and I can prepare hot meals for you and the rest of the garrison," Nanette urged. "All of you can fight so much better with hot food in your stomachs."

"Yes, Ma'm'selle, and let me go with Nanette," put in Jacques Brunet's mother steadily. "I can also milk the cows, and these children will be the better for it."

Touched by the sturdy women's thoughtfulness, Madeleine hesitated for only a moment. Then she gave her consent, and the two women hurried away.

The water casks in the blockhouse were empty, and Madeleine decided to tell Fontaine to have the two soldiers fill them with water from the well so that the women would not have to go for it. How wise her father had been when he had that well dug within the enclosure! Bringing water from the river would be a desperate undertaking now.

"The rest of you must stay here," she insisted. "Above all, do not let the children go outside the blockhouse for a moment."

With one thing and another the time passed so rapidly that, when she felt herself free, she knew that little of her rest period remained. She started for the manor house, intending to throw herself down on her bed for the short time that was left. She met Louis coming out.

"What time is it, my brother?"

He told her and added, "I woke and was afraid if I

went to sleep again I should sleep too long. I'm going to make the rounds of the palisades."

"I'll go with you," said Madeleine, thought of rest at once forgotten.

"You should be resting, but there is one place that worries me. This," Louis said, when they reached the place where the gap had been filled, "is the most dangerous spot in the whole stockade."

"The new pickets are strong and firm," Madeleine returned. "It wouldn't be easy to break through."

"To break through, no. The danger is in the bushes close up to the wall and in the gully just beyond. In the daytime from my bastion I can see into that gully fairly well, but at night a whole regiment might slip through and into the bushes and I would be none the wiser. If they once started to climb over—" He broke off, then added, "One or two might steal up here and set fire to the palisades. I tell you, Madeleine, those bushes must be cleared away."

"It would be too dangerous, Louis," Madeleine declared. "No one could do it without being seen."

"Not in daylight, but after dark it could be done," Louis told her. "Tonight I and someone else will go out there and cut down those bushes. You can guard us from the bastions. Even if the Mohawks hear our axes, they won't know what we are doing."

Madeleine was troubled. "It is a great risk, Louis."

"Not half as great as the one you took when you went down to the river to meet the Fontaines. Honestly, Madeleine, I think we run a greater risk in leaving those bushes there."

He was right, she knew. "Well," she said, "we will talk about it again before night comes."

Now Madeleine went to the post Fontaine was occupying on one of the rear bastions. There she seated herself on a stool and, her head against the wall, fell asleep. She did not sleep long, and when she woke, Fontaine urged her to rest longer. But she insisted on relieving him of the post he had held since early morning.

"The safety of the blockhouse depends on you," she said. "You must have sleep so that you may be alert all night. You had best go to the manor house. It is quieter there."

When Madeleine resumed her sentry duty, there was not an Indian in sight. The wind had gone down, the sky was almost cloudless, and on the open ground not a trace of last night's snow remained, though she could see white streaks at the edge of the woods. It had been so long since she had caught a glimpse of an Indian that she wondered if they had given up all idea of taking the fort, if they had moved on to attack elsewhere. She began to hope that the siege was over.

Her hope was short-lived. The sun was low in the west when a figure appeared from a patch of woods beyond the fields at the rear of the fort. He was followed quickly by another and another, a whole party of painted braves, almost naked, with heads shaved except for the scalp lock into which feathers and other ornaments had been braided. Single file, with long, loping steps, they crossed in the open just out of range. Without hope of hitting any of them, Madeleine raised her heavy musket to the loophole and fired to let them know they were observed. Almost at the same moment there was a shot from the blockhouse.

A stump was shattered, chips flying into the air. The warriors, without pausing, brandished their hatchets and firearms, yelled war whoops, and shouted what were doubtless insults and defiances. However, they did not turn toward the fort but kept on across the field and into the woods.

"They are gathering close about us for the night," Madeleine thought with a shiver.

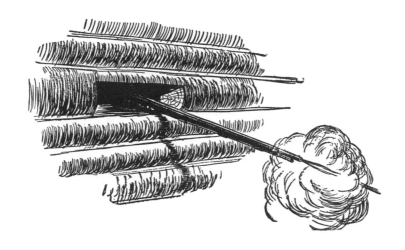

XII

A Daring Venture

AS DUSK DEEPENED, the smoke wisps rising here and there proved that the Iroquois were still camped around the fort. Within the palisades the approach of darkness was the signal for a vigorous renewal of noise and hubbub. Alexandre beat his drum to summon the garrison to night duty, orders were shouted, and as much clatter and racket made as possible.

The night was calm and clear, frosty but without the bitter chill of wind and storm. It was a far better night for sentry duty than the preceding one. A moving figure could be discerned long before it could reach the stockade, no matter how carefully it might steal from bush to stump. Sound carried far, too. There was no roaring of

119

wind or rattling of sleet to drown out lesser noises. The
Mohawks had let slip a valuable opportunity when they
failed to take advantage of the storm. On such a bright,
still night it would be almost impossible to reach the
fort without being seen, except by one approach. That
was in the shadow of the bushes that grew from the
very edge of the gully almost to the wall.

Louis remained firm in his determination to clear
away those bushes. With one other to help, he was
sure the work could be done in a short time. Who
was that other to be? La Bonté and Gatchet were out
of the question. Either one would refuse such dangerous duty. Alexandre was too small to handle an ax
effectively. There remained only Fontaine and Laviolette. Fontaine was Louis' choice, but Madeleine
hesitated to ask him.

"We must consider his family," she said. "It is
different with the rest of us. We have no one depend-
ent upon us. And besides, I don't want to take him
away from his post at night, even for a short time. I
feel that the blockhouse is safe only when he is on
guard. No, it will have to be Laviolette if he is willing.
He still handles an ax well, and he doesn't need as
much strength to cut bushes as to fell trees. But I
won't order him to such dangerous duty. If he volun-
teers, very well. If he hesitates, then I will help you
myself."

"You will do no such thing," Louis retorted hotly. "If
Fontaine cannot be spared, you surely cannot. Hon-

estly, I don't think there is any great risk if we do it as soon as full darkness comes. Between midnight and dawn it would be dangerous."

With this Madeleine agreed. Both knew that during the latter part of the night the Indians might be closing in for an attack.

When Madeleine told Laviolette of her brother's plan, the old soldier approved and promptly volunteered for duty. "I am an old man, Ma'm'selle," he said, "and I have neither wife nor child. Except that the garrison would be one less, it would not greatly matter if I were killed."

"It would matter a great deal, Laviolette," Madeleine returned warmly. "What should we do without you? You must be as careful as you can."

"Surely, Ma'm'selle, we will take every precaution. But M'sieu Louis is right. Those bushes must come down."

Nothing was said to Fontaine about the enterprise, but Madeleine told him that she wished to keep the two soldiers on the palisades during the early part of the night. When the darkness was as deep as it was likely to be, she took her station on the bastion that Louis had occupied, nearest the clump of bushes. La Bonté, who was a good shot, was on the opposite bastion, which, from farther away, commanded the same spot.

Louis had decided to climb the wall instead of going out at the gate. A narrow platform, one hand-hewn plank wide, ran around the inner side of the stockade, and to this platform a light ladder was raised. Madeleine watched, musket ready and heart beating fast, as her brother, sitting astride between picket points, balanced the ladder on the top of the wall and let it down carefully on the other side. Up there his head and body were exposed. Every instant she feared a shot from behind some stump or bush. But if he was seen, no armed scout lay near enough to fire at him. He placed the ladder, gave a hand to Laviolette, who scrambled up and over, and then descended himself without calling forth bullet, arrow, or war cry.

Madeleine drew a long breath when both were down in the shadow of the palisades. The greatest peril was just beginning, however. At that very moment, Indians might be lurking in the bushes or crouched in the gully beyond. The boy and the old man might be marching straight into a trap. She moved to another loophole that gave her a better view of the bushes and watched with straining eyes as the two slipped into the growth. The first ax stroke sounded alarmingly loud through the quiet night.

Not many strokes had fallen when there came a shout from the blockhouse. "What is happening there?" Fontaine demanded.

"It is all right," Madeleine called in reply. "Those are our own axes. All is well." She dared not divert her attention from the bushes and the gully long enough to explain.

Fontaine seemed content to wait for an explanation. He took up the cry, "All is well!" And the other
sentries echoed it.

From her post Madeleine could see the dark forms
of her brother and the old man slashing and crashing
among the bushes, hacking stout stems, slicing off
slender ones, breaking branches with their hands, and
treading them down with their feet. They were making
far too much noise, but noise could scarcely be avoided
if they were to do their work quickly. And there was no
time to lose. If they had been seen climbing the stockade, if the ax strokes and the cracking of branches
were heard by the enemy scouts, then enemy warriors, even now, might be crawling up the gully.

Tense with fear, Madeleine watched that shallow
rift, trying to peer into its shadows. She thought she
saw something moving down there. It seemed as if the
darkest part of the shadow was shifting a little. Her
grasp tightened on her musket. She opened her lips to
shout a warning. But there was no further suggestion
of movement. Her eyes had deceived her.

How long the task was taking! She knew that Louis
and Laviolette were working as fast as they could, but
it seemed to her that they had been down there a long
time, and the work was not half done. She must not
think of that. She must watch, watch, her eyes, her
ears, her mind concentrated on the gully. To watch the
gully was her special task. La Bonté had been instructed
to scan the open ground between the fort and the

woods, to look for Indians creeping from cover to cover, to be on the alert for any sign of danger from that direction. The young militiaman had not made a record for bravery, but he seemed impressed with the importance of this duty. He could be trusted, she thought, to keep a close lookout and to sound a warning if he saw danger approaching even though he might run away afterward. She was forced to trust him, for her whole attention must be given to the gully and its immediate surroundings.

The clearing away of the bushes went on without interruption. There came a time when Louis was hacking at the last large bush, and his companion was slicing off and breaking down the smaller growth on the very brink of the gully. Suddenly, Laviolette uttered a sharp exclamation and disappeared. Madeleine gasped with horror. She saw Louis spring to the spot. But already the old man was scrambling up.

A musket roared from La Bonté's bastion. With one stroke Laviolette brought down a small shrub. Louis felled his bush and flung it into the open. Then he ran for the wall, the old man after him.

Madeleine dared not move back to the other loophole to watch them climb over. It was not her part to watch *them* but to keep her eyes on the place from which danger might come. She knew what was happening, of course. Louis must be balancing himself on the top of the palisades while he drew up the ladder.

*Louis felled his bush and flung it into the open. Then
he ran for the wall, the old man after him.*

And what had La Bonté fired at? She dreaded to hear another shot.

"All safe!"

Madeleine's musket, which she had been holding so steady, trembled in her grasp. For fear of dropping it she set it down against the wall. She tried to answer Louis, but her voice was gone.

She was still facing the loophole. Suddenly, she saw something that brought her to herself, that tightened all her slack muscles. Up over the rim of the gully a head arose. She could see it plainly now that the bushes were down. She waited until shoulders followed the head. Then she seized the pistol that lay, loaded and cocked, on the stool at her side and fired.

The head and shoulders dropped back. Had she hit the man or only frightened him? She discarded the pistol, raised the musket, and waited. To her ears came the pad of moccasined feet. Louis was running to join her.

"What was it?" he cried. "What did you shoot at?"

"A Mohawk, climbing out of the gully," gasped Madeleine.

"Did you hit him?"

"I don't know. He disappeared. Oh, Louis, if he had come a few moments earlier—"

"But he didn't come," said Louis with satisfaction. "He was too late. We've been lucky."

"Not merely lucky, Brother. Truly your guardian angel has protected you. Thank God you are safe!"

"Yes, Madeleine," agreed Louis. "It is done and over. That gully is still a bad place, but they can't get from it to the fort now without being seen—not unless it's black as pitch. And it won't be that dark tonight. I'll take my old post and keep an eye out for the fellow. If you didn't kill him, he may try again."

"I'll stay here too for a while. Where is Laviolette?"

"Gone to relieve La Bonté," Louis told her.

"La Bonté must have seen something or he wouldn't have fired. What happened to Laviolette out there?" Madeleine asked.

"He slipped and fell in, but he didn't hurt himself."

"I was frightened," Madeleine explained. "I thought someone had pulled him down into the gully."

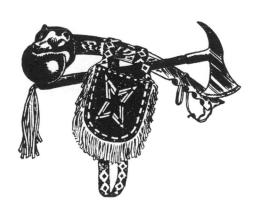

XIII

Waiting and Watching

WHEN THE EXCITEMENT of her brother's daring venture had subsided, Madeleine began to feel the results of some forty hours of wakefulness. In two days and nights she had taken only that one short nap in Fontaine's bastion. Now she began to realize that she was very weary in body and mind. In the calm and stillness of the night she grew overwhelmingly sleepy. But even stronger than her desire for sleep was her fear that she might give way to it. She moved back and forth from one loophole to another, forcing her tired eyes to examine carefully every foot of ground visible under the clear, starlit sky, compelling her drowsy mind to take note of everything. At frequent intervals she started the cry of "All is well," her voice so husky with weariness that it might easily be taken for a man's. Around and around went the cry, four or five times, before silence settled down again, to be broken in ten or fifteen minutes by another round of shouts.

So the night dragged on, Madeleine fighting an unceasing battle against weariness and fear. Suddenly, light footsteps ascending to her bastion startled her. As she turned her head, there came a gleam of light. "Who is it?" she cried, conscious as she spoke that no Indian would carry a lighted lantern.

"Here is supper for you, Ma'm'selle." It was Nanette.

"Nanette, you ought not to leave the blockhouse at night. Weren't you afraid?"

"Yes, Ma'm'selle," Nanette replied simply as she set her basket of food on a stool. "But I knew you must be hungry. Madame Brunet came with me, and M'sieu Fontaine sent La Bonté to guard us. He is out there now with a basket for M'sieu Louis. Madame Brunet is in the kitchen preparing other baskets for M'sieu Sandre and Laviolette."

"It is brave of you, Nanette," Madeleine said, touched by the girl's devotion, "brave of both you and Madame Brunet. I *am* hungry, and I know the boys must be. This will give us strength for the rest of the night's watch. But you must go back to the blockhouse just as soon as you can. What time is it?"

"After midnight, Ma'm'selle."

Though Madeleine felt hungry, she found herself able to eat but little. She was too tired. What she did succeed in swallowing strengthened her, but it did not relieve her desire for sleep.

Since she had fired at the head emerging from the gully, she had not caught sight of a moving object. Not even a rabbit had hopped across the open. The night was so still that scarcely a bush was stirred by the breeze. The only sounds that came to her ears from outside the stockade were the rippling of the river and the occasional hoot of an owl from the woods. But she knew all too well that the peace and silence were deceptive. The Mohawks had not gone.

She must keep awake until sunrise, and she must make sure that no other sentry fell asleep at his post. Twice when the cry of "All is well" went the rounds, Alexandre was slow in taking it up, and once Louis was tardy in response. Her brothers, like herself, were struggling with drowsiness.

The sky began to lighten at last; the stars paled. Dawn came, and still the Mohawks made no move. Another anxious night was almost over.

"Ma'm'selle Madeleine," Nanette's voice was calling, "your breakfast is ready, and M'sieu Fontaine is coming to relieve you."

When Fontaine arrived, Madeleine was glad indeed to give up her post. She went straight to the manor house, which she had entered only once since the first alarm. It seemed strange to find everything the same in the kitchen. Had it been only two days since she had helped Nanette to prepare breakfast, and she and Louis had talked of his escapade with Jacques Brunet? Where was poor Jacques now?

Alexandre, relieved by Gatchet, was at the table before her, and they breakfasted together. The little fellow looked exhausted.

"Don't you suppose the Mohawks have gone away?" he asked.

"I fear not, Sandre," said Madeleine sadly. "Just because they don't show themselves does not mean that they have gone. One did show himself early in the night." And she told him then about the Mohawk she had seen crawling out of the gully.

"Why don't they attack us then?" asked Sandre. "I should think they would at least try to find out if they can storm the fort."

"No doubt they would if we hadn't convinced them that it is well defended. If they thought we were sleeping—speaking of sleep, my brave little brother, you must go to bed at once."

Madeleine half-led, half-carried the little fellow to his bedroom and left word that he was not to be wakened until afternoon.

Dropping with weariness though she was, Madeleine did not go to rest until all the sentries had breakfasted. Then she slept with the soundness of exhaustion. In less than four hours, however, she was awake. The moment she opened her eyes, her anxiety and sense of responsibility returned. She rose and went out to make the rounds of the defenses.

Everything was in good condition. But from the sentries she received disturbing reports. Indians had been sighted several times at the edge of the woods, and three well-loaded canoes on the river had been recognized as Iroquois craft. Two parties of warriors had passed the rear of the fort and, safe out of musket range, had shouted defiance. No shots had been fired by the defenders. Fontaine and Louis had agreed that the guards were not to fire unless someone came within easy range.

Before she resumed her post, she paid a visit to the blockhouse, gave out the rations, and spoke encouragingly to the women and children. She was relieved to find Madame Fontaine less tearful though still very much afraid.

Her rest had shortened the day for Madeleine, and the afternoon passed swiftly enough. The movement of the Indians, their sudden appearances on all sides of the stockade, kept the guards continually on the alert. One tall, broad-shouldered fellow, fantastically painted with zigzag stripes of red and black and with a bunch of red feathers in his scalp lock, was seen several times, now on one side of the fort, now on another. His appearance was so striking that everyone noticed him. Every glimpse of that hideous warrior left on Madeleine a particularly threatening and sinister impression. She wondered if he was the leader of

One, fantastically painted with zigzag stripes of red and black, was seen several times.

the band, or at least of that part of it left to watch the fort.

The approach of darkness found the whole force on duty again—Madeleine, her brothers, and Laviolette on the bastions, Fontaine and the militiamen in the blockhouse. The sentries were thankful that again the night was clear. The restless movements of the Indians had made the little garrison very apprehensive. Everyone felt that the enemy was growing impatient and would be ready to seize the first favorable opportunity to attack.

Yet hour after hour passed uneventfully. With the darkness the Mohawks seemed to have settled down. Midnight came and all was quiet. Without relaxing her vigil, Madeleine ate her cold lunch of bread and cheese. She had forbidden Nanette and Madame Brunet to leave the blockhouse during the night.

Now dawn drew near, and still not an Indian showed himself. Madeleine had grown so used to sentry duty by this time that her eyes kept watch while her thoughts wandered. Especially she thought of her father in Quebec, completely unaware of what was happening in his seigneury, and of her mother in Montreal, making haste to finish her business, anxious to be at home again. Had she heard of the raid? Had the Iroquois approached Montreal? Had news of their presence along the river reached that town?

A new and terrible fear clutched at the girl's heart. Perhaps her mother, ignorant of any danger, was even now on her way down river. Perhaps she had already been waylaid and was at that very moment in the hands of the Mohawks. If there were only some way to reach her, to warn her—if she had not yet left Montreal—of the trap in wait for her!

Madeleine tried to reassure herself. Her mother had been away but a short time, not six days, and the girl doubted if the business could yet be completed. Surely Mother could not have started for home. By the time she did start, the Mohawks would be gone, or word would have reached Montreal of their doings. Then she would come with troops to rescue her children and the seigneury. With such thoughts Madeleine strove to reassure herself.

As a matter of fact, there was no one Madeleine could send with a warning even if there had been the slightest chance of his getting through. She could only pray for her dear mother, pray from the depths of her heart that God would guard her and keep her from falling into the hands of the Iroquois.

Determinedly she tried to put these new fears out of her mind and to devote her whole attention to her task. Her brothers, the fort, and the seigneury were her responsibility, and the peril of the dawn was at hand.

Once again dawn brightened into day without alarm. The sun rose, and Nanette's voice sounded cheerful, almost happy, as she summoned the weary sentries to breakfast. They went two at a time.

After Madeleine had breakfasted, she visited Louis' bastion. "Has all been quiet along the gully?" she asked.

"All quiet as far as I could see. I believe those Mohawks are a pack of cowards, Madeleine. They outnumber us ten to one, yet they are afraid to attack."

"They don't know they outnumber us so greatly. I doubt if they are cowards. They are trying to wear out our patience."

"Playing with us like a cat with a mouse," said Louis, frowning at the woods.

"Yes, waiting until we grow careless or fall asleep on guard. When that happens, they will strike and strike quickly."

"It's our affair to see that doesn't happen," said Louis stoutly. "This is the hardest thing I ever tried to do, Madeleine, this waiting, waiting. I almost wish they would attack and get it over. If we could only make a sortie and fight, it wouldn't be so bad."

"I know how you feel, Louis, but there is nothing we can do," Madeleine told him, "nothing but stand fast and watch that they do not catch us napping. Go and have your breakfast, Brother. It will put new heart into you."

XIV

The Fire Bearer

THE FOURTH DAY of the siege differed little from the third. The besieged had grown accustomed to their routine. Each knew his duty and did it. The women in the blockhouse went about their work and took turns standing guard. To the babies it mattered not at all where they were so long as they were fed and comfortable. The older children had adapted themselves to the changed conditions and played and squabbled as usual. The sentries slept when off duty and kept an alert lookout for signs of danger while on their bastions.

As on the day before, Indians were seen from time to time, especially the tall warrior with the zigzag stripes, but they seldom came within musket range. And al-

ways the sentries felt, even when there was not an Indian in sight, that the fort was closely watched.

The weather was warmer, with a gusty wind and
alternating clouds and sunshine. Behind heavy clouds
the sun went down, bringing darkness early. The overcast sky and deep blackness increased the dangers of
the night. It would be much easier for the enemy to
steal close to the wall since the sentries were forced to
depend less on sight and more on hearing. Eyes and
ears were strained to the utmost, peering into the blackness for moving shadows, listening for stealthy footsteps, for the click or rattle of a weapon, for any sound
with a threat in it.

Trying to pierce the darkness in the direction of
the gully, Louis was thankful that he had not delayed
clearing away the bushes. On such a night as this,
that tall growth would have furnished perfect con-
cealment. With the bushes gone, it might be possible
for night-accustomed eyes to make out a moving figure
stealing or crawling from the edge of the rift.

He was congratulating himself on the removal of
the cover when he became conscious of a moving
object. It was coming from the gully—swiftly, noise-
lessly. He raised his musket, took hasty aim at the
moving black mass, and pulled the trigger. The flint
struck the steel lid of the priming pan, but the sparks
from the impact failed to reach the priming powder.
The musket mis-fired. He dropped it and seized a pistol. The pistol did not fail him, but the object, still

indistinct of outline, came on. He had missed his mark. The thing darted forward under the overhang of the bastion.

Lois flung away the empty pistol, reached for another musket, and went down on his knees beside a hole in the floor. In the deep shadow below, he could at first make out nothing. Then—yes, there was a spot blacker than the shadows. To his dismay, he discovered that the musket he held was not cocked. It was the same one he had tried a few moments before! Fearing it would mis-fire again, he dropped it and groped for some other weapon. Never once did his eyes wander from the hole.

Suddenly, a spark of light glowed below. In a moment it became a tiny tongue of flame. Something moved just as his fingers closed on a second pistol, but he was too late to fire down on the creature. As a musket roared from Madeleine's bastion, he sprang to his feet. Regaining the loophole from which he had first seen the thing, he sent a shot after a running form that had left its trail of fire behind. Without its burden of inflammable stuff, that form was a man. To prove further its human character, it let out a savage yell of defiance as it disappeared into the gully.

"Look, Louis, flames!" Madeleine shrieked.

He did not need to be told. He had seen the fire start. Smoke was coming up through the holes in the floor.

Louis laid aside his pistol and started to go for

water. Then he stopped short. Was the kindling of the fire a genuine attempt to burn the stockade? More likely it was only a ruse to draw him away from his post for a few minutes. Perhaps the enemy wanted to attract all the defenders to this one spot while they attacked elsewhere.

As he hesitated, Fontaine called from the block-house, "What is wrong there?"

"They've tried to set fire to the palisades. I dare not leave my post to get water."

"Don't leave. I'm coming," shouted Fontaine. Obedi-ently Louis went back to his loophole and picked up another musket, which, loaded and cocked, was lean-ing against the wall. He was just in time to see a myste-rious mound—perhaps hay or branches—being rushed toward the stockade. This time he was more cool, his aim was better, his finger steady on the trigger. The flint struck the priming-pan cover sharply, the cover fell back, the sparks dropped on the powder. The musket bel-lowed, and the mound went down, remaining motion-less.

His eyes on the barely discernible heap on the ground, Louis reloaded. If only he could clearly see the object of his aim! Terror of the unknown threat almost overwhelmed him. If it had been daylight, if he could have seen the man clearly as he fell, his sensations might have been different. But that black thing out there was a freshly sinister sort of peril, a danger that was cruelly threatening.

Throwing back his shoulders, Louis concentrated on the mound. Was the heap stirring a little? Yes, part of it was moving now—not toward the stockade but back toward the gully. The man had dropped his load and was creeping away. Before Louis could fire again, the crawling figure was absorbed by the blackness.

The fire was now burning vigorously. Smoke was pouring through the floor, and the smell of burning pitch mingled with that of gunpowder. The flickering light penetrated the gloom beyond the bastion. But Louis stood to his post. He must keep eyes and thoughts on the darkness beyond that wavering light.

Fontaine, carrying two buckets of water, was not long in coming. He emptied one through the hole in the floor, and Louis, who had not turned his head, heard the hissing as water struck flame. The second bucket followed. The light flickered out. But Fontaine was taking no chance. He hurried away for more water.

"It is out now," he declared when he had again emptied the pails. "But this has taught us something. We must keep water on every bastion. How was the fire started?"

"A savage came up out of the gully," Louis explained. "He had his arms full of something, branches or dry grass. I fired at him and missed. Then he ran in close to the wall, and before I could get another shot, he had lighted the pile. He was quick about it. He must have been carrying live coals and tinder daubed with pitch."

"Well, he is not likely to try it again tonight, not in

the same place, anyway," declared Fontaine. "But we must be ready here and everywhere. I am going to refill these buckets."

Carrying out his plan for the distribution of water, Fontaine took one of the buckets to Madeleine's bastion. "The fire is out," he assured her, "and no harm has been done. The pickets may be scorched a little, that is all."

Madeleine urged him to return to his post at once. "They may try to set the blockhouse on fire," she said, "and you know La Bonté and Gatchet are not to be trusted where there is real danger."

"They are doing better," Fontaine replied, "especially La Bonté. I won't leave them alone long, but I want to take water to all the bastions."

"Do so then, and warn Laviolette and Sandre to watch for other attempts to set fires. Be as quick as you can, Monsieur."

The attempt to fire the stockade, made so early in the night, proved plainly, if proof were needed, that all the Mohawks were not sleeping.

"God grant us help soon," prayed the girl commander as she strained her eyes to see out into the blackness. "If they really attack us in force, it will be the end. The blockhouse can be saved perhaps, but all else will go—Louis, Sandre, and I with it."

A sick feeling of discouragement and fear overcame her for a moment. Was this the last night? Would the sun rise on the wrecked and smoldering ruins of the fort of Verchères?

"All is well! All is well!" Fontaine's shout, echoed by Louis, broke in upon her despair.

Sturdily, Madeleine took up the call. It was no time for the commander to be disheartened. Whatever moments of weakness she had endured in private, she had succeeded so far in hiding her fears and doubts from the rest of the tiny garrison.

If the Indians had wanted to increase the vigilance of the defenders, they could not have hit upon a better method than their attempt to fire the palisades. All night long, shots from both the blockhouse and the bastions indicated that some sentry thought he saw a figure moving among the still shadows of shrubs and stumps and stones. More than once Sandre beat his drum furiously. Cries of "All is well" rang constantly through the blackness.

Just before dawn when, as usual, the tension was redoubled, Madeleine, peering out of a loophole, felt something on her face. It was a misty rain. Her lips formed a prayer. Any fire that the enemy started now would be quenched speedily. As the light grew stronger, the rain strengthened also, falling steadily without wind.

The night had passed, and the fort still stood. Its defenders were alive and uninjured. Before another sunset help might come.

XV

The Refugee

THAT WHOLE DAY was wet and dull. Low-hanging gray clouds covered the sky, and rain fell intermittently. The woods looked dismal. Fields and meadows were soaked. The St. Lawrence was wrapped so completely in mist that a whole fleet of canoes could have passed without being seen by the sentries in the fort.

As far as the little garrison could see and hear, there was much less activity among the besiegers than on the day before. From the time when Madeleine came on duty, after her few hours of rest, not a single Indian was glimpsed by the sentries.

Late that afternoon the sky began to clear. A cloudless night dotted with innumerable stars followed the brilliant sunset. On no other night since the siege began had the range of vision been so good.

The air grew sharp and frosty. Even in woolen hose and moccasins, feet chilled quickly when not in motion, and it was no easy task to keep fingers limber enough to handle musket or pistol. But what if the comfort of a fire was unknown except during hastily snatched meals? What, too, if every throat was hoarse with shouting and every eye strained with watching? These were small things compared with fire, torture, death. No one thought to complain of them.

Hour after hour of darkness passed without alarm. Not a living creature but a solitary rabbit hopping across the starlit clearing, and an owl, calling from the woods, was either seen or heard. So far as the guards could tell, clearing, fields, woods, and river were void of human life.

The quiet and silence made it doubly hard to keep awake and alert. Twice before midnight Madeleine realized with horror that she had slipped off into a doze. After this she started the cry of "All is well" at even more frequent intervals than during the previous night. Sometimes the tardiness of a response alarmed her, but everybody, even Sandre, fought successfully the battle against drowsiness.

Midnight passed without alarm, and time dragged slowly on. As the stars waned in a paler sky, the sleepy sentries forced themselves to greater alertness. Still there was neither sight nor sound of human beings outside the walls.

Following her regular routine, Madeleine went to visit Louis immediately after breakfast. He was standing at a loophole, but his body and head had sagged against the wall. At her step he straightened up, but his eyes met hers a little sheepishly.

"Another night gone, my brother," she said cheerfully.

"Yes, and I believe the Mohawks have gone with it. Did anyone see or hear anything during the night?"

"No, I have asked them all. There was not a single alarm."

"They have gone," Louis asserted positively.

"I hope so indeed," his sister told him, "but this quiet may be only a trap to lure us outside the walls. We must be very careful."

"Of course," he agreed, "they're not going to catch us napping. Still, this morning for the first time I'm going to sleep in peace."

Had the enemy really gone? Or was the quiet of the past twenty-four hours only a snare? Until she went off for her rest period, Madeleine weighed hope against fear. But after hours of refreshing sleep, it was hope that tipped the scales for her. Nobody had seen or heard an Indian. Not a wisp of smoke had risen from woods and fields. A flock of little gray juncos were feeding on weed seeds close to the palisades. They hopped about, rose in the air, wheeled, and lighted again—fluttering, scratching, picking up seeds, uttering squeaky chirps. The tiny creatures seemed quite carefree and unafraid. Surely there was nothing hidden behind stumps and bushes to frighten them!

Late in the afternoon Louis came to visit his sister in the bastion overlooking the gully. "Madeleine," he sang out jubilantly, "I've just thought of a way to find out whether those fiends have really gone or whether they're just trying to trick us. Listen to my plan."

He had spoken only a few sentences when Madeleine's eyes began to grow big with excitement. "Wonderful, Louis! How clever of you to think of it! Hurry. Bring the things and we'll rig it up in no time."

"All right. But first I'll run and tell the others what we're doing."

A few minutes later, a soldier's hat with a gallant cock's feather appeared suddenly over the rim of the palisades. Dauntlessly, as if this had been night instead of broad daylight, the unseen wearer of the hat swaggered along between two bastions. Madeleine held her breath. Not a shot greeted the daring fellow. He was almost halfway between the bastions now. Yes, it was true. Surely the Mohawks had gone; otherwise, they would have aimed promptly at this promising target.

P-s-st! With the hiss of that bullet, Madeleine's brief joy turned to despair. The hat ducked but rose a little farther on and drew fire again.

"Shall I try it on the other side?" Louis cried.

"There's no need. If they are on this side, they are all around us." There was a note of discouragement in the young commander's voice.

The brave head in the hat with the rooster's feather did not appear above the pickets again, though it would have been no great loss to the garrison if it had been hit. It was only a pumpkin head on a stick. Close by, it would have deceived no one, but the Mohawk outposts were not near enough, though within musket range, to see through the hoax.

Louis carried the uninjured hat back to his sister. "Well, anyway," he said grimly, "we know now, don't we?"

"Yes, we know now." Mechanically Madeleine took the soldier's hat from him and jammed it on her head. It was the same one she had worn all through the siege.

Another night of suspense and watchfulness lay ahead. And what it would bring no one could tell. Only one thing was certain: vigilance must not be relaxed. When Madeleine made a short visit to the blockhouse, she found the women bitterly disappointed, for all had begun to believe the danger past. The children had begged to be allowed to play out of doors, and the mothers had felt Madeleine overcautious in refusing to let them do so even within the palisades. Now they knew she was right. She tried to make them laugh by describing Louis' trick, and her brave spirit heartened all but Madame Fontaine, who lay weeping on her bed and refused to be comforted.

It was only a pumpkin head on a stick.

The defenders had hoped for another clear night, but with darkness a strong veering wind blew up while clouds came and went across the sky. The voice of the roughened river grew louder, and Madeleine could hear its waters slapping up against the log dock. Wild gusts whipping around the bastions lifted and banged every loose object in the stockade. This was even more terrifying than the storm of the first night.

To no one was the stormy night more of a test than to Alexandre. Even in peaceful times, when no threat of death hung in the air, he always stayed close to Louis on nights like this. For to him these were the night winds that witches loved. They rode on their cloud racks. Their voices were one with the gale that whipped and rattled—quiet one moment only to be fiercer the next. But now—wistfully he thought of the blockhouse. All the habitant boys and girls were there. Yes, of course, they were frightened. But at least they had company.

Suddenly, a shot! It had come from the blockhouse. Since dusk Sandre had seen nothing of the enemy, and it was now after midnight. But *someone* had just seen something. He listened for more shots, but no further sound came.

Running first to one loophole and then to another, he peered into the storm. A cloud directly overhead made the darkness so deep that he could see scarcely anything. But the cloud was sailing before the wind. It passed on, and when the shadow was gone, a creeping figure, stealing along close to the stockade, was revealed.

Sandre raised his musket. The heavy thing was all he could handle, and its powerful recoil nearly felled him every time he fired it. Perhaps it was dread of that kick that made him challenge before firing. *"Qui vive?"* he cried in his deepest tones. "Who goes there?"

"Sandre, don't shoot!" a husky voice replied breathlessly in the Norman French that nearly all the habitants used. "It's me, Jacques Brunet."

Sandre knew the voice. "Jacques! You got away!"

"Quick! Can you let me in?" panted Jacques.

"What goes on there?" came Laviolette's shout from the opposite bastion.

"It's Jacques Brunet," called Sandre. "We must let him in."

"Tell him to keep close to the wall, to go around to the gate and wait in the shadow," commanded Laviolette at once. Then the old man called out, "Ma'm'selle, Ma'm'selle, Jacques Brunet is outside. Is it your will that the gate be opened for him?"

Madeleine could scarcely believe her ears. "Keep your post, Laviolette," she cried, "and watch the gate. I will open it."

Louis heard his sister say she would open the gate but had not heard the reason for it. Had relief come at last, or was this some trick? Determined not to let her take any more lonely risks, he shouted, "Wait, Madeleine, I'm coming."

She did not hear him. Before he could join her, she had unfastened the gate and opened it a crack. "Jacques," she said in a low voice.

A musket from the woods answered, and a bullet buried itself in the stout log gate. Laviolette fired from his bastion overlooking the gate just as Jacques slipped through the narrow opening.

At that moment Louis ran up. In the darkness he could see only that someone had come in. "Just one?" he asked as he sprang to help Madeleine close the gate.

"Louis! It's me," said a well-known voice, husky with strain.

"Jacques! Where did you come from?"

"From the Mohawk camp," replied Jacques. "We escaped, Antoine and I."

"Then where is Antoine?" Louis asked fearfully.

Jacques' reply brought new hope.

"Gone to get the soldiers from Sorel."

After the gate had been made fast, Madeleine ordered, "Run back to your post, Louis. Jacques, your mother is in the blockhouse. Go to her."

"Wait, Ma'm'selle, wait!" implored Jacques. "I have news—terrible news. The Mohawks are attacking at dawn. They are getting reinforcements."

"How do you know, Jacques?" asked Madeleine.

"A mission Indian told me, and I'm sure he was not lying."

Madeleine thought quickly. It was now just past

midnight. Five or six hours must pass before the attack. "Go straight to your mother now, Jacques," she commanded. "Relieve her mind at once but say nothing of your news to anyone in the blockhouse. Then come to my bastion and tell me everything."

"My bastion must be manned," Louis said. "Shall I try to get La Bonté?"

"No, go back, and I will come to you there when I have heard Jacques' story, and we shall decide together what is to be done."

Both boys went on the run. As they left the shadow of the palisades, Louis saw that Jacques was bare to the waist, and his breeches were in rags.

Before returning to her own post, Madeleine called up to Laviolette, "Did you see the man who fired?"

"Yes, Ma'm'selle. I hit him, I think. He went down, and I've seen nothing more of him. The boy is not hurt?"

"No, but he had a narrow escape. Good work, Laviolette."

As she hastened back to her bastion, Madeleine thought with a heavy heart how little they could do to prepare for the coming attack. But Antoine had gone to the King's fort at Sorel. God grant that he might bring help speedily!

XVI

Warning

IT WAS NOT LONG before Jacques joined Madeleine on her bastion. Someone had given him moccasins and a leather shirt, but he was still shivering with cold and fatigue.

"Oh, poor Jacques!" she murmured. "You have had little time with your mother, and no rest. But please—quick—tell me all you know."

In breathless sentences he poured out his story of how he had been seized by the Mohawks and had met Antoine, who had been captured the previous night.

"How did the Indian come to tell you of their plan?" interrupted Madeleine.

"He was not friendly, just boasting," Jacques explained. "He must have been a poor Christian, for he

154

is as heathen now as the others. He speaks a little French, so they set him to find out from us how well the fort is defended."

"What did you tell him?"

"That there were more than twenty soldiers here with plenty of ammunition," said Jacques. "I feared if I made the number too great he wouldn't believe me, but I knew the savages would be in no hurry to try to storm so strong a fort with twenty well-armed men defending it."

"Do you think he did believe you?" Madeleine asked.

"I wasn't sure at first. Next morning he asked Antoine, and Antoine said twenty-five men. The fellow nodded and answered that he thought there must be many soldiers from the noise they made."

"Good! Then our shouting was not in vain. Do they still believe the place is well defended?"

"Oh, yes," Jacques told her. "They have been afraid to attack while you were wide awake and watching for them. They have been waiting to catch you off your guard. This morning the mission Indian came to me again. He wanted to know if the seigneur himself was here. 'Yes,' I told him, but he laughed and said the seigneur was far away with Onontio. I knew I had made a mistake, but I tried to look innocent. I answered that the seigneur had been in Quebec with Onontio—Governor de Frontenac—but had returned the day before the Mohawks came. Then Antoine spoke up and said that the Sieur de Verchères had brought news that the Governor himself would soon be coming up the river with hundreds of soldiers.

"I don't know whether the fellow believed us that time or not. He boasted that Onontio would be too late to save the fort. 'More warriors come to join us before the sun goes down,' he said, 'and before it rises again the fort will be destroyed.'

"I didn't know what to say, but Antoine took the news more coolly. 'So you think you're going to attack tonight, do you?' he asked. The way he said it, sneering as if he didn't believe they had the courage, made the Iroquois angry.

" 'Before the dawn comes,' the savage declared, 'when most of the soldiers are sleeping, we go to take the fort. We will kill all the men and take away the women and burn the houses. Onontio will come too late.' "

Madeleine felt her blood growing cold. Something dry constricted her throat, and she swallowed hard before she asked, "Did he mean it or was he just tormenting you?"

"He meant it, I'm sure," said Jacques despondently.

"And did the warriors come?" Madeleine asked sharply. She must know at once just how bad the situation was going to be.

"That I don't know. We were kept over on the other side of the woods where we couldn't see or hear what was happening. I think the party they expected was one that went from here several days ago down river to raid."

"How did you manage to get away?" Madeleine's voice was somewhat more calm now.

"We couldn't get a chance during the day. We were bound, and they untied our arms only when they brought us food," went on Jacques. "And all day there were some of them in sight. But when night came, we seemed to be alone. So Antoine rolled over to the fire and got his wrist cord against a live coal and burned it through. Then he untied his ankles and came and untied me."

"But how did you get through their lines?"

"It wasn't easy," Jacques admitted. "We had decided that Antoine should try to get clear away and bring the soldiers from Sorel or wherever he could find them. I was to slip into the fort and warn you of the attack. So he went along the river's edge, under the bank, while I circled back through the woods. I wanted to reach that gully out there and creep through it, but there were so many Indians along the creek I had to go away up above the mill before I dared try to cross."

"It was lucky for you that you didn't reach the gully," Madeleine told him. "There are scouts in it all the time."

"I was nearly caught more than once. I had to creep very slowly and lie in wait to cross the open places until the clouds covered the sky. It took a long time. M'sieu Fontaine shot at me from the blockhouse."

"Have you told Monsieur Fontaine about their plans?" Madeleine asked.

"No, Mademoiselle Madeleine. You told me not to say anything of my news in the blockhouse."

"That was right. Thank you, Jacques."

Leaving Jacques in her own place, Madeleine went to Louis. Their consultation was short. They agreed that the other sentries and Monsieur Fontaine must be told at once about the threatened attack, but there was no need of frightening the women in the blockhouse. If the attack came, they would know soon enough. All the firearms had been distributed to the bastions and the blockhouse and were kept loaded and ready for use. On each bastion also were buckets and tubs of water. One other means of defense they had, but how could they avail themselves of it?

"I wonder," Madeleine said, "if there is any way to raise La Bonté's courage to such a point that he can be trusted to stay out here and take charge of the cannon. He is the only one who knows how to fire it."

"I can fire the cannon, Madeleine," Louis said confidently, "and Jacques can take my place here. He is far more dependable than La Bonté. He has shown that tonight."

"But you have never fired a cannon, Louis!"

"I have watched. I'm sure I can do it," insisted the boy.

"You might blow yourself up," said Madeleine slowly. Then, after a moment's silence, she added decisively,

"If La Bonté will come out here now, before anything happens, and show you just how to do it—"

"All right," Louis interrupted. "We'll try him. Shall I go and tell the others about the attack?"

"I will go. Louis," Madeleine laid a hand on his shoulder, "we must not deceive ourselves. If the attack really comes and we stay out here, there is only the faintest chance that we can frighten the savages away. If they are at all determined, they will soon overwhelm us. Perhaps we can retreat to the blockhouse. We will if we can. But it is more than probable that we shall not have time to reach it if the fight goes against us."

She paused, and he replied promptly, "We know all that, Madeleine. We have known it from the first. We can't do anything but stay here and do our best."

"Well spoken, my brave brother. I knew you would feel that way."

"And so will Sandre," Louis added. "He does get afraid sometimes, but he goes through with things, just the same. He is as brave as anyone when his mind is made up to do a thing."

"I know he is, Louis. We'll see it through then, for our country, our King, and our God."

"And the honor of Verchères," Louis added.

With a heavy heart but a brave and determined bearing, Madeleine went on her rounds, feeling her way in the deep shadow of the palisades. Laviolette had little to say. Most certainly he would stay at his post.

When his sister told him the terrible news, little Alexandre could say nothing at first. He was trying to hide the fear in his heart. But when she hesitatingly suggested that he take refuge in the blockhouse, he was indignant.

"Maybe I'm not as brave as you and Louis," he declared, "but we Verchères are not cowards, and if you are going to stay out here and fight, I am, too."

"Don't you think we ought to stay, Sandre?" she asked, to give him a chance to express his opinion.

"Why, of course," he exclaimed as if he had not thought anything else possible. "Of course we must save the fort if we can. Perhaps if we make a great deal of noise," he added, "they won't dare come."

"We will do our best, little brother."

Alexandre drew a long breath and said stoutly, "I have thought a good deal, Madeleine, about what might happen to us. But I don't think I am really afraid to die here with you and Louis. Father Dollier says God is merciful to those who are brave and do their best. He said it to Mother, you remember, after François was killed. François did his best, and we are doing ours."

Madeleine was glad that the darkness hid the tears in her eyes as she kissed the little fellow. "They may not come at all, Sandre. That mission Indian may just have been boasting, or Antoine may bring help in time. God keep you, my brave little brother."

Not wishing to be overheard by any of the women,

she called Fontaine into the passageway. Once again he urged her to forsake the stockade and retreat to the blockhouse. But when he found her firm in her refusal, he insisted that he should join her on the bastions.

Again Madeleine overruled him with the same arguments she had used before.

"The fate of the women and children rests with you, Monsieur," she said earnestly. "You know that Gatchet and La Bonté are not wholly to be trusted. Whatever happens, you must defend the blockhouse." When he continued to protest, she added firmly, "Monsieur Fontaine, as long as you remain in this fort, you are under my orders. You are a man and I am only a girl, but while my father and mother are away I represent them. For the time I am the head of this seigneury and the commander of this fort, and I am determined to be obeyed."

"As you will, Mademoiselle. I am under your orders."

"That is settled then. As to telling La Bonté and Gatchet, perhaps it would be as well to keep them in ignorance until the attack comes. But I want La Bonté for a few minutes. Louis wishes to learn to fire the cannon. We may frighten the enemy away with that."

"A good idea, Mademoiselle," approved Fontaine. "Indians are always terrified at cannon. If we had such a gun to command each side of the fort—"

"But we haven't, so we shall have to do our best with one. Will you send La Bonté at once, Monsieur?"

Jacques begged to be allowed to remain on guard.

If Louis was to act as gunner, another sentry was needed, so Madeleine consented to let Jacques stay. Privately she made up her mind that, on his mother's account, she would find some pretext to send him with Sandre to the blockhouse as soon as the attack began and would instruct Fontaine to keep them there.

La Bonté arrived promptly, carrying a lantern. By the feeble light of its candle, he showed Louis how to load and aim the little cannon and to set off the charge with a lighted fuse. He warned the boy to avoid the recoil by stepping back quickly after applying the fuse and cautioned him not to reload until the gun had cooled somewhat. Rapid firing with such a crude muzzle-loading weapon was impossible.

"The best way to be sure you understand is to do it all yourself while I stand by and see that you do it right," said La Bonté self-importantly.

To this Louis had no objection, for he was eager to fire the gun. "It will do no harm to give those Mohawks a fright," he said.

To the great surprise of the women and children in the blockhouse and doubtless of the waiting, watching enemy as well, the cannon soon boomed forth into the night. La Bonté waited until it was cool enough for reloading and watched Louis perform that task. Before leaving he asked the boy why he had chosen this time for a lesson.

"Is it that you have some reason to think there will be an attack tonight?" he questioned.

"Oh, you can never tell," Louis returned in as casual a voice as he could muster. "They may try it any time. It occurred to me that if they did come, I might make some use of the cannon. But my sister wasn't sure I knew how to handle it. As soon as I got the idea in my head, I couldn't wait till morning. Who knows what may happen before dawn?"

XVII

Brave Hearts Await the Dawn

ALL POSSIBLE preparations having been made, there
was nothing to do but wait. Since the shot at Jacques as he entered the gate, the enemy had not been
seen or heard.

Cries of "All is well" were sent around and around,
the handful of watchers trying to vary the tones of
their voices. Lights were shown here and there, and
each sentry tramped about, clattered his weapons,
shouted questions and answers, and made all the
noise he could. When he thought dawn must be approaching, Alexandre beat his drum for several minutes. Noise was still the main defense, though no one
felt any great confidence in its power permanently to
protect the fort.

The wind, which had steadied, blew away most of the clouds. Slowly the sky grew lighter. The minutes crept by. To the four sentries on the bastions, the waiting, with taut nerves and courage screwed to its highest point, grew well-nigh unbearable. Almost incessantly they shouted back and forth. The cry of "All is well" seemed a mockery now. But to make a noise, to hear answering voices, was a slight relief to the overstrained nerves of each lonely guard.

Still nothing happened. Not a moving thing was to be seen. Not a shot was fired. Not a war whoop was raised. Dawn drew near, but still everything around the fort was as quiet and deserted as if there were not a Mohawk within miles. As the light of day strengthened, hope grew in every heart.

At last, dawn came. The sun was up. The sixth night of the siege was gone, and the fort was still untaken. Suddenly, Madeleine found herself so weary she could scarcely hold her body upright at its post. The reaction from the tense strain left her weak in every muscle. When Fontaine came to take her place, she answered his greeting mechanically and went her way to the manor house like a sleepwalker.

Breakfast revived her a little, and she made an effort to be cheerful when Sandre joined her. But he was in no condition to notice how she looked or what she said.

Three or four times he fell asleep over his food. As soon as he had managed to eat a little, Madeleine sent him to rest.

Madeleine dropped off to sleep the moment she lay down and slept heavily. She woke with a start and the feeling that she had far outstayed her time, but when she went to consult the clock, she found that she might have lain still for another quarter of an hour. Her sleep had refreshed her less than usual. She was still very weary and slack and dull-minded. How much longer could she hold out, through how many more dragging days of anxiety and sleepless nights of fear? For the first time she felt that she had nearly reached the limit of her strength, and the thought frightened her. In the cold, deserted living room, she sank down in a chair—a handsome armchair that had come from old France—buried her face in her hands, and gave way to tears, weariness, and disheartenment.

The closing of the back door aroused her. Nanette or Madame Brunet had come to prepare the noon meal. They must not find her crying. She stood up, wiped her eyes, straightened her disordered dress, glanced at the clock, and went quickly out of the house by the front door. Scarcely noticing anything around her, she sought the little log chapel. Into the cold, close, dimly lighted room she slipped and knelt before the altar, where the long candles burned steadily. She prayed for strength and courage to carry her trust through to the end, whatever the end might be, and added petitions for speedy succor and relief and for her mother's safe return. Comforted and strengthened, she rose and went about her duty.

She gave way to tears, weariness, and disheartenment.

Madeleine returned to the manor house and aroused her brothers. Then she went directly to the bastion overlooking the gully where she found Fontaine, who had exchanged places with Jacques.

Fontaine reported considerable activity among the Indians. "I feel, Mademoiselle," he said, "though I can't quite explain why, that something new is going on around us. I believe they are planning something."

"Unless the fellow who talked to Jacques was lying," Madeleine returned, "they planned something for last night, yet they did nothing."

"And there is the reason why," Fontaine cried. "Look!"

Swiftly she took his place at the loophole, which gave her a view of part of the fields and meadows at the rear of the fort. Crossing the clearing, the sun shining on their painted bodies and glinting from their musket barrels, knives, and hatchet-tomahawks, were warriors, a long line of them.

"That is the party that was expected yesterday. They didn't come, so the attack was postponed, but tonight—"

Madeleine interrupted him. "They are coming straight toward the fort! No, they are turning off to the woods."

"They will make no general attack by day," Fontaine declared.

The sight of that war party, the realization that last night's great peril had merely been postponed, brought Madeleine's heart close to utter despair. But, as before, she was determined not to betray weakness.

"Before night, rescue may come," she asserted stoutly. "Surely the whole country cannot be ignorant of what is happening here. Someone must come to our aid soon."

"True, Mademoiselle." Fontaine was glad to encourage her. "Much may happen between now and midnight."

Louis appeared at that moment, and Fontaine took his departure.

"So that is the reason they didn't try it," said Louis when his sister told him what she had just seen. "I hoped they had given up the idea. Madeleine, how much longer can we hold out?"

It was the question she had been asking herself with no certain answer. But she did her best to reply encouragingly. "We have provisions for a long time, and a fair supply of ammunition if we don't waste it. As to fuel, we are not so well stocked. If we are besieged a month, we shall have to begin tearing down the houses for wood to bake our bread."

"A month! This siege can't last that long!" exclaimed Louis.

"No, Louis, I'm sure it can't. News of our plight must reach Montreal or Quebec. Then Father or Mother will bring troops to our relief. But I must go at once. Jacques is in my bastion, and he too must have rest. Courage, Brother, help may be close at hand."

Doubtless Fontaine had been right about the unusual activity during the morning, but after the return of the raiding party few Indians were to be seen. Whether they were lying quiet in the woods or scouring the country in small bands, leaving only hidden scouts to watch the fort, there was no way to tell. Whatever they were doing, their plan to attack, Madeleine was convinced, had not been abandoned but merely postponed. She had spoken bravely of rescue before night, but as hour after hour passed without change in the situation, her hopes faded. Antoine could not have reached Sorel. Less lucky than Jacques, he must have been killed or recaptured.

XVIII

Sounds from the River

THE SUN SET behind clouds. All day the weather had been uncertain, and now a raw east wind threatened rain or snow. With that persistent feeling almost of despair, Madeleine realized that the night was to be a dark and probably a stormy one. She was the last to eat her supper, and as she sat at the table before the fire in the kitchen, her mind was busy with the problems of the coming night.

Nanette, who was moving about her tasks, interrupted her thoughts. "I am thinking, Ma'm'selle—"

"What is it, Nanette?"

"The night will be cold. You and the young gentlemen and old Laviolette will need hot food. Let me take it to you at midnight, Ma'm'selle Madeleine—a good, thick soup of pork and peas and cabbage and carrots."

"No, Nanette," Madeleine replied firmly. "You must stay in the blockhouse. Is that the soup there on the fire?"

"Yes, Ma'm'selle."

"It smells good. It would put new heart into us, I have no doubt." Madeleine paused and considered.

There was little chance that the Mohawks would attack until well after midnight. Just before dawn would be the time. It seemed strange to think of food when in a few hours her brothers, the old servant, and she herself would probably be dead. But they were all very weary now. They would feel the chill of the raw weather. At least they might have the comfort of a warm meal.

"Don't cover the fire too deeply, Nanette," she directed. "Leave the kettle of soup simmering on the coals. We will come, one at a time, for a bowlful. But you must go back to the blockhouse and stay there until morning."

"Yes, Ma'm'selle, I will leave everything ready." Nanette knew nothing of the threatened attack.

Except for the rushing of the wind, the swishing and rattling of dry bushes and bare-branched trees, the incessant muttering of the river, all outside the stockade was quiet. Inside, the shouts of "All is well" were kept going. Useless the noise might be if the Indians were really resolved, but to keep it up was the only thing the defenders could do except to strain eyes and ears in the attempt to pierce the danger-fraught blackness.

When midnight came, Madeleine told Louis to go to the manor house and eat a good meal. After eating, he relieved Laviolette. Sandre was the third to have his midnight supper, and then Jacques. To Jacques, Madeleine gave instructions to take a generous portion of the stew to Fontaine and the two soldiers.

Madeleine was the last to go, Jacques taking her place. Carrying her heavy musket to be ready for any alarm, she made her way through the darkness, her feet dragging with weariness, her body trembling in the chill wind. The threatened rain had not yet come, but not even in the sleet and snow of the first night of the siege had she felt the cold so keenly.

She laid her musket on the kitchen table, stirred up the fire, and crouched over it to warm her chilled body. Then, with a long-handled wooden ladle she served herself a bowlful of the thick broth. Nanette had left bread to be eaten with the soup. A mouthful of the hot stew aroused Madeleine's appetite. She ate slowly, listening to the cries muffled by the thick log walls of the manor house, "All is well. All is well." The comforting warmth of fire and soup was creeping through her tired body.

She ate the last spoonful, pushed the bowl from her, and debated in her sleepy mind whether she wanted more. There was still a little in the kettle. No, she did not want any more soup, but she did need a few more moments of warmth and rest—only a few moments. Her eyes closed, her head drooped, her body sank forward. Arms outstretched on the table, head resting on them, she was sound asleep.

"Mademoiselle Madeleine! Ma'm'selle!"

She started up. The door was open; the cold wind was blowing in and flickering the candle flame.

It was Jacques who was calling her. "Ma'm'selle, come quickly."

She seized her musket and ran out. "What is it, Jacques?"

"I don't know, Ma'm'selle. Laviolette heard something down by the river. He challenged, but there was no answer. Then he told me to come for you. I, too, thought I heard something." They were running across the enclosure as Jacques explained.

A shout came from Louis. "What is it? Are they coming?"

"Laviolette has heard something from the river. Keep your post, Louis. Go back to your place, Jacques. I will join you in a moment."

She mounted Laviolette's bastion and groped her way to him where he stood trying to see out toward the river. "You heard something?"

"I thought so, Ma'm'selle. The clink of a musket striking against a stone. Listen," the old man whispered. "Your ears are young."

He moved aside, and she took his place at the loophole. The darkness was so black her eyes could make

Arms outstretched on the table, head resting on them,
she was sound asleep.

out nothing, but to her ears, in a lull of the wind, came slight sounds, rustlings, clickings, then a voice, low-pitched, speaking a word or two. Were the Indians closing in? She must know at once. She could not endure this waiting.

"*Qui vive?* Who are you?" she shouted.

The reply came from close at hand. Its nearness startled her almost as much as the words. "Friends. We come to bring you help."

Madeleine's whole body was trembling. Help? Rescue? She did not dare believe. She heard old Laviolette murmuring over and over, "Ma'm'selle, Ma'm'selle," in a shaking voice. But she remembered the renegade mission Iroquois who spoke French. Could this be a trap?

"What friends?" she demanded, trying to speak firmly and boldly. "Where are you from? Who is your leader?"

"It is La Monnerie," the voice replied promptly, "La Monnerie, at your service, Mademoiselle de Verchères. De Callières sent me."

La Monnerie, sent by De Callières, Governor of Montreal! There could be no doubt now. But even in her relief and her joy, Madeleine did not forget courtesy. Nevertheless, her voice trembled in spite of all efforts to steady it, as she said, "You are most welcome, Monsieur de la Monnerie. The gate shall be opened at once."

"My men are down by the river, Mademoiselle. I will bring them up."

Bidding Laviolette follow, Madeleine hastened down to unfasten the gate. By the time she had it open, she had gained better command of herself. La Monnerie's men were not so quiet now. From the direction of the river came voices and the rattling of equipment. Scarcely realizing what she did, she went out through the gate and toward the river to meet the advancing relief.

So dark was the night that she could see nothing of the approaching men. And she stopped short in sudden surprise when a black figure loomed directly in her path. Holding herself stiff and still, she raised one hand to her hat in salute. "Monsieur de la Monnerie?"

"Mademoiselle de Verchères! All is well with you here?"

"All is well, Monsieur. To you I surrender my arms and the command of the fort."

"No, no, Mademoiselle. It is in good hands, I am sure."

Madeleine smiled to herself in the darkness. What he said was mere gallantry. He did not know what her little garrison had been through. "Better perhaps than you think, Monsieur," she replied proudly.

Led by La Monnerie and the girl, the soldiers filed through the open gate where old Laviolette stood with his musket at attention. The weapon shook and wavered as his tired old arms trembled, but he held his head high.

"Have you seen anything of the Mohawks, Monsieur?" Madeleine asked when all were inside and the gate was closed.

"Our scouts came in contact with theirs, Mademoiselle, but we knew nothing of how it was with you here. We feared greatly that Verchères had been taken. So we approached cautiously. The enemy, warned of our coming, disappeared before us."

"They can't have been gone long," Madeleine told him. "Only a few hours ago they were all around us. They must have withdrawn in the darkness. We did not see or hear them go."

"They are like that, Mademoiselle," replied La Monnerie. "One moment you know them to be close at hand. The next they are gone, and you have heard nothing. When we saw all so dark and silent here, we feared we had come too late."

"Had you come a little earlier, you would not have found it so silent." As she described how they had kept up the shouts of "All is well," it seemed strange that the approaching troops had heard nothing. Then she remembered the rushing and roaring of the wind and knew that the calls of the sentries could not have carried far above that noise.

"Our only chance," she went on, "was to make the Mohawks believe this place well defended."

As La Monnerie listened to Madeleine's explanation, he looked about in puzzlement. "Where is your garrison, Mademoiselle?" She had come out alone to meet him, and as yet he had seen only her and the old man at the gate.

"I will show you, Monsieur," said Madeleine with a tired smile. "Will you come now and inspect our defenses? But first I will bring a lantern that you may be able to see your way."

Carrying the lantern herself, she led La Monnerie along the palisades. "The women and children," she told him, "are all in the blockhouse with three men to guard them. The blockhouse is strong and well provisioned. It could hold out for a long time."

Louis, at his post, had not been unaware of the arrival of help. But he came of a family of soldiers. Like Madeleine, he was determined that the newcomers should see that all was as it should be, that the tiny garrison was standing to their arms. Eager as he was to be at his sister's side, he held firmly to his duty. He would not leave his post until he was relieved. So he saluted and stood stiffly at attention as Madeleine and the officer approached.

"This is my brother, Louis," explained Madeleine to La Monnerie proudly. "He has been my lieutenant and next in command all through the siege."

"It is unusual to find an officer doing sentry duty," remarked La Monnerie, looking with keen interest at the slender boy with rumpled hair, tired face, and hollow eyes.

"But you see, Monsieur, officers are about all we have here," Madeleine replied, smiling.

Then she led La Monnerie to the next bastion where he found another lad of about the same size, a ragged, broad-faced, shock-headed habitant boy. It was the faithful Jacques.

"Are all your sentries half-grown boys, Mademoiselle?" the bewildered officer asked as she led him on.

"Not quite all. You can scarcely call this next one a boy." It was old Laviolette, who had returned to his post as soon as the gate was closed.

To the leader of the relief party the greatest surprise of all was the occupant of the fourth bastion. Like his elder brother, Alexandre drew himself up and saluted in a soldierly manner. Had the candle lantern given a stronger light, it might have shown a moistness in La Monnerie's eyes as he gazed at the gallant little lad with the big musket.

La Monnerie turned to Madeleine. A queer figure she made in her man's hat and heavy rough cloak, a smudge across one cheek, and her eyes big and dark with weariness. "Mademoiselle de Verchères," he said, "I don't understand. Your guards—where are they? Madame, your mother, said she had left ten men with you."

"Two of those men are in the blockhouse under our neighbor, Monsieur Fontaine. Luckily he got to us the first day of the siege. But for the rest—" and she plunged into the story of the militiamen's hunting expedition that had led not only to their own capture but to that of all the male habitants.

Open-mouthed, the officer gazed at her, and it was a few moments before he could speak. "How can one take in such a story?" he murmured at last. "All this time we in Montreal have had one comforting thought. Ten militiamen—at least they were here to protect you. Instead, you and three small boys and one old man have held off the Mohawks for a week!"

She smiled faintly. "Two small boys, M'sieu. It was only last night that the habitant boy came back to us."

La Monnerie whipped off his hat and swept it to the floor in a low bow. "Mademoiselle de Verchères, I can find no words tonight for your exploit. But tomorrow, perhaps by then I can think up some tribute worthy of your bravery."

"You will remain then, M'sieu?" asked Madeleine in profound relief.

"We shall make this our headquarters. Of course, you understand, we must scout up and down the river. We must see to it that not a single Mohawk is left on the south bank of the St. Lawrence. But now, Mademoiselle, you and your garrison need sleep. Rest peacefully. Tonight no evil thing can happen in Verchères."

"Yes, we shall sleep—my brothers and I and dear, brave Laviolette. God has been good to us, M'sieu."

XIX

Madeleine Resigns Her Command

LA MONNERIE and his forty men took over the defense of Verchères. The Mohawks had withdrawn from the immediate neighborhood, but as yet no one knew how far they had gone. The seigneury could not be considered out of danger.

Madeleine was too tired to ask many questions. When La Monnerie had assured her that Montreal had not fallen and that her mother and the little ones were unharmed and would return to Verchères as soon as Governor de Callières would permit, she did not ask more.

Her only wish was for sleep, and there was no longer any reason why she should not take it. The Indians would not attempt to storm the fort now that it was so well defended. Yes, she could sleep securely. For the first time in a week she dared to undress and go to bed, without concern as to how long she remained away from her post.

She did not wake next day until late afternoon. Looking out through the small leaded panes of her window, Madeleine could scarcely realize that the past week had not been merely a bad dream. The enclosure was no longer quiet and deserted. The women, with their babies and belongings, had returned to their cabins. Smoke rose from the chimneys, children were playing about, voices came through the open doors. A group of La Monnerie's men had gathered about the blacksmith shop. And from the kitchen below Nanette's voice, cheerful as a bird's, trilled:

> *"Elle s'aperçoit d'une barque*
> *De trente matelots,*
> *De trente matelots,*
> *Sur le bord de l'ile,*
> *Sur le bord de l'eau."*

> "She caught sight of a bark
> With thirty sailors,
> With thirty sailors,
> At the shore of the island,
> On the bordering waters."

"Nanette," she called down, "will you bring me hot water, please?"

"It is ready for you, Ma'm'selle, and also for the young gentlemen," called back the cheerful voice.

"And will you tell the young gentlemen, Nanette, to put on their best clothes tonight?"

"I have already told them that such is Ma'm'selle's wish," answered Nanette. "Also, I have had Laviolette build the fire in the living room and set the table there."

"And our guest, Monsieur de la Monnerie? Has he returned yet from his scouting?"

"Not yet, Ma'm'selle, but all in good time. I told him this morning of all the good things we were taking from the storehouses in his honor. Never fear, Ma'm'selle, but that a man will come back for such a dinner."

The hot bath for the first time in a week gave Madeleine a sense of great luxury. She dressed carefully and combed her long hair, matted for so many days under her soldier's hat. When at last she came down the stairs, it was in her buckled shoes, and her long skirt and the red jacket which her father had brought her from Quebec.

Laviolette rose from his stool by the kitchen fire as she entered. He, too, had been transformed from the unkempt old man of the past week into the neatly attired servitor who had always greeted his master's children at their evening meal.

"Ma'm'selle," he said, "it is good to see you so again. I have been wondering as I sat here—was it all a nightmare?"

Madeleine's face grew swiftly grave. "For us who are still safe and sound—for us who have lost no dear ones—yes, Laviolette, it is only a nightmare. But think of all our cabins tonight. The fires are burning, the suppers are cooking, the children are playing. Yet what a change! Husbands and fathers are gone. Can you imagine my father's grief when he hears about his people—about Jacques Brunet's father?"

"Ma'm'selle, Ma'm'selle, do not give way to such thoughts. Tonight is for thanksgiving. You have behaved magnificently as the commandant. Now you can be the seigneur's daughter again. And how proud the seigneur will be of his daughter!"

"I hope you are right, Laviolette," she began.

Louis' voice called her name excitedly from upstairs.

"Yes, Louis, what is it?"

"It's Antoine! They've rescued him. I can see him from my window."

She ran to the door and flung it open. In the gathering dusk a tall young man limped toward her, accompanied by one of the soldiers.

"Antoine!" she cried.

"Mademoiselle Madeleine, what can I say? I failed you and Verchères. Imagine how I felt when the savages described their plan to kill—"

"Don't speak of the past, Antoine," interrupted Madeleine. "You have suffered for your recklessness. Thank God you have come back. Tonight, as Laviolette says, we must rejoice and give thanks. Go to your mother at once. She has been so brave through all her anxiety for you."

"The women and children of Verchères have served you better than some of us men," he said gravely. "But I will make amends, I promise you."

"You will, I know, Antoine, and there remains much to be done."

"I go now to reassure my mother but will return soon to report to my commander." He caught up her hand and kissed it.

"Rather to Monsieur de la Monnerie, to whom I have gratefully resigned my command."

When Antoine had left, Madeleine went to the living room where Nanette had spread the table with the finest linen and highly polished silver and glass.

To La Monnerie, when he entered and saw his hostess standing there in the candlelight to receive him, she seemed a vision indeed. Could this be the weary, dirty girl who had welcomed him the night before?

He saluted with military formality, then bowed low over her hand. "A brave commander, Mademoiselle de Verchères, and may I say, a most charming lady as well."

"I must have been a droll figure indeed in that soldier hat and my old cape," said Madeleine, smiling.

"A gallant figure," he amended. "You have proved yourself an able and valiant commander, Mademoiselle, and you, Messieurs Louis and Alexandre, have

shown equal courage and determination in supporting your leader. The whole of New France is in your
debt."

La Monnerie spoke earnestly. His words were not
mere gallantry, but sincere and from his heart.

"Had this fort fallen, the Indians would have been
encouraged to attack the others more fiercely, and it
might well be that none but the strongest, such as the
King's fort at Sorel, would be standing now. The valor,
the determination, the clever strategy you have shown
here have saved your neighbors as well as yourselves."

Madeleine's cheeks were red with mingled pleasure and embarrassment, and the two boys glowed
with pride. "You praise us too much, Monsieur," the
sister said. "We tried to do our best. In honor we
could do no less. But," her voice trembled a little,
"we could not have held out much longer. Had they
attacked us last night—and they would have attacked,
I am sure—the fort must have fallen. God in His mercy
permitted you to come just in time, Monsieur de la
Monnerie."

As they sat at the dinner table, once more a digni-
fied seigneurial family entertaining a distinguished
guest, the conversation centered almost entirely upon
the siege. Eagerly La Monnerie inquired about every
detail of the defense. Eagerly the three defenders un-
folded their experiences, each adding particular acts
of the heroism of the others. Madeleine's sortie to
the Fontaines' rescue was told, Louis' feat in clearing

*Eagerly La Monnerie inquired about
every detail of the defense.*

the approach to the gully, and best of all, they said, was Sandre's drumbeating to confound the enemy.

On the whole, the meal was a pleasant one. A really happy one it could not be, with thoughts of the killed and captured recurring in the minds of all.

Madeleine turned to entreat the officer: "Monsieur, do you think there is any chance of rescue for our poor captured ones?"

"You know, Mademoisclle, that a large part of my command is even now scouring the country. I have hopes, too, that the Christian Iroquois at the mission of Sault St. Louis—"

"Christian Iroquois!" interrupted Louis. "What can one hope from them? Haven't you heard, Monsieur, about that renegade Indian who questioned Jacques and Antoine? I would never trust any mission Indians. They always turn on us in the end."

"No, Louis, that is not quite true," returned the officer gravely. "You are very young; you have just gone through a terrible ordeal at the hands of the Indians. Naturally enough, you detest them all. Yet some of the Iroquois who become Christian do stay Christian. Time and again they have helped us in our campaigns. Hasn't your father told you the same thing?"

"Of course he has—and Laviolette, too," Madeleine said.

"Well, certainly it would be a great jest if our people had to be rescued from the Indians by the Indians." Louis turned defiantly from the officer to his sister.

"It is a jest that has been played more than once in New France," replied La Monnerie. "And believe me, if your people are returned, it will probably be by those good Indians at the mission of Sault St. Louis. It is well said that only an Indian can find an Indian, and only an Indian can fight an Indian."

Soon after this the commandant rose to take his leave. It was necessary for him to be out at dawn with his searching parties, and his young hosts certainly needed more sleep. The three young people rose and gave their stiff salute. La Monnerie returned it before going to Madeleine's place at the head of the table.

"Mademoiselle de Verchères," he said, "the Governor of Montreal will soon know of your magnificent feat. And it won't be long before all Quebec is ringing with it, too. I have no doubt but that our great Governor de Frontenac will write you his appreciation as soon as he hears the story of your heroism."

When La Monnerie had gone, Madeleine laid a hand on Louis' arm as he started to leave the room. "There is one thing still to be done, my lieutenant."

"Have you not resigned your command, *mon capitaine?*" he inquired mischievously.

"Forever, I hope," Madeleine said laughingly. "But have you forgotten your sword? I would like to restore it to you."

"I wondered if you had forgotten it."

"Let's make a ceremony of it," cried Sandre. "I'll get my fife."

"*Mon capitaine,* I thank you."

"And call Nanette and Laviolette," Madeleine said. "They were here when Louis surrendered it."

A minute later the door swung open. Piping an old French tune on his fife, Sandre led the way into the living room. Meanwhile, Madeleine had gone to a cupboard and taken from it Louis' hunting knife. Echoing the fife, Nanette and Laviolette came in singing. As they finished the verse, Madeleine came forward with the knife.

"My lieutenant, I return to you your sword, brighter now than ever before."

"*Vive* M'sieu Louis!" cried the three watchers as Louis received his knife.

He looked at it before he plunged it into its sheath at his belt. Then gravely he saluted his sister. "*Mon capitaine,* I thank you."

XX

Peace Once Again

BENEATH THE SOFT blue of the sky, the river flowed
as peacefully as though its waters had never been
lashed by sweeping winds or fretted by pelting hail. A
blue-white haze softened the deep green of the spruce
and pine, the winter brown of the oaks, and the black
penciling of bare-branched trees on the islands. The
sun had gone down, for November days are short in
the north country. In the west where the tender blue
merged into pale green, low-lying clouds were tinted
with rose and lavender and mauve. After the late October rains and the squaw winter of sleet and snow
and heavy frost, had come in November a few days of
true Indian summer, of calm, mild, delightful weather.

How beautiful it all was, quite as beautiful as in
midsummer, Madeleine thought as she stood looking
out at the scene. In contrast with the browns and yel-
lows, the tans and grays of ripened foliage and bare

branches, of withered weeds and grass, the blue of the river was more vivid than in summer when all was green. And how peaceful it was! The contralto voice of a chickadee perched in a red-stemmed, leafless dogwood bush sounded cheery and unafraid. A bold, black-and-white woodpecker hammered undisturbed on the log wall of the bastion.

The long days and longer nights of fear and dread did indeed, as old Laviolette had said, seem like a nightmare. With the arrival of the soldiers and the scouting and patrol measures they had taken, the hostile Indians had quickly disappeared from the banks of the St. Lawrence and the Richelieu.

Madeleine knew well that peace and security might not last indefinitely, but just now she was not thinking of what might happen in the future. She had far pleasanter things to think about. When the sun was setting she had climbed to the bastion near the gate. As she stood at a loophole looking up river, she felt how different this watching was from the fearsome vigils of the siege. Then she had watched in dread for a savage enemy. Now, in hope and confidence, she was looking for her own dear mother. The evening before, a messenger had come down river from Montreal with word that Madame de Verchères had finished her business there and would leave at once for home. She might be expected some time the next day, the messenger had said.

All day Madeleine and her brothers had been on the

*Now, in hope and confidence, she was looking
for her own dear mother.*

lookout. Now the sun had set, yet their mother had not come. Madeleine was not worrying about her, however. She felt that Madame de Verchères, not yet sure but that hostile Indians might still be lurking somewhere in the woods along the river, would not risk exposing the little children to the risks of night travel and so could scarcely reach home very early in the day.

No, Madeleine was not worrying but thinking with a happy heart of the events of the day that was passing. Only a few hours before, one of the Verchères habitants who had been at Quebec in military service with his seigneur had arrived with a letter from her father. Word of the gallant defense of the seigneury by his daughter and two sons had reached the father through Pierre Fontaine. Fontaine, after the immediate danger was over, had yielded to the entreaties of his timid wife and had taken her and the children to Quebec to remain until she could be assured that they would be safe in their island home.

"I feel Monsieur Fontaine praised us too highly," Madeleine had said after she read the letter to her brothers. "Father seems to think we have done something wonderful."

"You have been wonderful, Madeleine," Louis had insisted. "I don't believe anybody, even Father, could have commanded better. Sandre and I just obeyed orders."

"You did more than that, both of you, far more," his sister had returned warmly, laying a hand upon the shoulder of each. "I'm proud from the bottom of my heart of my noble brothers, and so are Father and Mother. You were not only brave and steadfast and willing to take any risk. You used your wits. Father says that he is proud not only of our courage but of our strategy. That strategy was as much yours as mine, Louis—more, I think. How about the pumpkin head in the hat? And Alexandre kept his wits too and used them. He thought of the drum." She had smiled tenderly at the younger boy.

"Well," Louis had said, reddening a little, "we all did our best, I guess. And so did Laviolette and Jacques, and everybody but La Bonté and Gatchet." The lad was immensely pleased and proud at his father's praise, but he did not want to show his pride too plainly.

"Maybe La Bonté and Gatchet couldn't help being cowards if they were born that way," Alexandre had suggested. "I was afraid myself, lots of times," he admitted. "If I had been just a little bit more afraid, I might have run and hidden in the blockhouse, too."

"Not you, Sandre," Louis had snorted. "You're a Verchères."

It was of the letter and of her father, as well as of her mother, that Madeleine was thinking as she looked out upon the river. A small canoe was in sight a little way out. Louis and Alexandre were paddling about in what appeared to be an aimless manner. Suddenly, they swung the birch craft about and began to paddle vigorously. They were making for the landing.

Madeleine needed no other signal. She hurried down from the bastion, and before the boys' canoe reached the landing, she was running down the rough path.

"They're coming," Louis shouted.

Scarcely had the boys made a landing when two canoes came in sight around a bend, not too far away for the eager watchers to make out the red cloak of Angélique in the one and the familiar bonnet of Madame de Verchères in the other. Louis and Alexandre pulled off their caps, waved them around their heads, and shouted, but Madeleine stood still, her heart beating fast.

The men in the leading canoe slowed their paddling and let the second one pass so that it might reach the dock first. As it came alongside, Louis knelt and seized the bow. The stern paddler held the canoe close up to the dock and another of the *voyageurs* stepped out to assist Madame de Verchères and little Jean.

The lump in her throat still prevented Madeleine from making a sound, but when her mother's arms clasped her in a warm embrace, the girl who had come through great peril and strain with a steadfast heart broke down. She was not in the least ashamed of the tears that brimmed over and ran down her cheeks. *Maman* was at home, *Maman* and the little ones! They were all together again, safe and sound, all except Father, and he had written that he hoped to come soon.

Epilogue

OVERLOOKING the St. Lawrence, where it sweeps around a sharp bend, some twenty miles by water below Montreal, stands the bronze figure of a young girl, a sturdy, alert, determined girl, bearing a musket. The statue is that of Madeleine de Verchères, the heroine of this story. The courageous Madeleine is not a mere character of fiction. She was a real flesh-and-blood girl, who, with her younger brothers, actually held, as related in this tale, the fort of Verchères against raiding Iroquois. Louis and Alexandre were real, too, and took their part gallantly in the heroic defense. The fort and the manor house are gone long since, though there is a village of the same name in what was, when

Canada was New France, the seigneury of Verchères. But the old days are not forgotten. The statue on guard above the river commemorates the heroic feat of the sister and brothers. The story of that feat is one of the thrilling chapters in the glorious history of Canada.

History has little more to tell us of the seigneury and the family of Verchères. La Monnerie proved correct in his prophecy that the Christian Indians might be able to trail the raiders though the soldiers failed. The Mohawks slipped away out of his reach, but a band from the Iroquois mission of Sault St. Louis at the head of the St. Louis Rapids near Montreal came to help in the search and were more successful. They got on the trail of the main party of the raiding Mohawks and overtook them on Lake Champlain. There the mission Indians recovered more than twenty prisoners, most of them from Verchères. Then there was rejoicing indeed in the families of the liberated habitants.

Governor de Frontenac was firm in his determination to rid New France of the Iroquois menace. To carry the war into their own territory he sent that winter a great expedition against the Mohawk towns. The towns were taken and burned, and a battle was fought with a combined force of Iroquois and English, in which neither side can be said to have triumphed. In the meantime a truce had been declared between France and England. So for a time the war between the French and English colonies ceased, though four more years passed before a treaty of peace, the Treaty of Ryswick, was signed in Europe.

In the seigneury of Verchères the winter of 1692–93 was not without its dangers, but a fair harvest had been gathered and there was no starvation. The Easter festival, with the seigneur at home, was a happy one, and no one was happier than old Laviolette. How he loved to tell over and over again, to anyone who would listen, the story of the siege!

The following summer, the Ottawa and the St. Lawrence were again opened to trade, and another great fleet of friendly Indians came down to Montreal. Ships with soldiers and supplies arrived from France. More prosperous and less dangerous days were coming to the frontier country along the upper St. Lawrence.

While it was several years before the peril from Iroquois marauders was really over, Verchères does not appear to have ever been seriously threatened again.

Louis and Alexandre grew up to take their places among the noblesse of New France and, like their father and elder brother, served their King and country well. Madeleine, we can be sure, developed into an able and a charming woman. History says that she married, and that for her service to her country in holding Verchères against the Iroquois she was given a life pension. At the request of Monsieur de Beauharnois, a later Governor of New France, she related the story of how she withstood the Iroquois. Whether she wrote it out herself or one of the Governor's clerks set it down on paper as she told it, we do not know. However it was recorded, her brief account has come down to us. And on that account is based this tale of how a fourteen-year-old girl and her twelve-and-ten-year-old brothers, aided only by the old servant, the settler Fontaine, and the two none-too-brave militiamen, held the stockaded fort of Verchères for a whole week against the Mohawks.

Bibliography

In French:

BARBEAU, M., and E. SAPIR, *Folk Songs of French Canada* (French and English).

CASGRAIN, H. R., *Une Paroisse canadienne au XVIIe siècle.*

———, *Legendes canadiennes et variétés.*

CHAPAIS, T., *Jean Talon, intendant de la Nouvelle France.*

FAILLON, M. E., *Histoire de la colonie française en Canada.*

FERLAND, J. B. A., *Cours d'histoire du Canada.*

GAGNON, ERNEST, *Chansons populaires du Canada.*

GARNEAU, F. X., *Histoire du Canada.*

GASPÉ, P. A. DE, *Les Anciens Canadiens.*

GIBBON, J. MURRAY, *Canadian Folk Songs* (both French and English).

LORIN, HENRI, *Le Comte de Frontenac.*

MASSICOTTE, E. Z., and C. M. BARBEAU, *Chants populaires du Canada.*

ROY, R., *Le Régiment du Carignan.*

SAGARD, G., *Histoire du Canada.*

SULTE, B., *Histoire des Canadiens-Français.*

———, *La Noblesse au Canada.*

———, *Le Régiment du Carignan.*

TANGUAY, C., *Dictionnaire gènealogique des familles canadiennes.*

In English:

Along Quebec Highways, Tourist Guide.

BARBEAU, M., *Folk Songs of Old Quebec.*

BESTON, HENRY, *The St. Lawrence.*

BOUCHETTE, JOSEPH, *A Topographical Dictionary of Lower Canada.*

BURPEE, L. J., *Historical Atlas of Canada.*

BURT, A. L., *The Old Province of Quebec.*

CALL, F. O., *Blue Homespun.*

——, *Spell of French Canada.*

CHARLEVOIX, F. X., *History of New France.*

COLBY, CHAS. W., *Canadian Types of the Old Régime.*

——, *The Fighting Governor.*

DOUGHTY, A. G., *A Daughter of New France.*

DOUGLAS, JAMES, *Old France in the New World.*

GARNEAU, F. X., *History of Canada,* translation by Andrew Bell.

GREENOUGH, W. P., *Canadian Folk Life and Folk Lore.*

HALE, KATHERINE, *Canadian Houses of Romance.*

KALM, PETER, *Travels into North America.*

KINGSFORD, W., *History of Canada.*

LA HONTAN, BARON, *New Voyages to America,* Thwaites edition.

LE MOINE, J. M., *Chronicles of the St. Lawrence.*

MUNRO, W. B., *The Seigneurs of Old Canada.*

——, *The Seigniorial System in Canada.*

PARKER, GILBERT, and C. G. BRYAN, *Old Quebec.*

PARKMAN, FRANCIS, *Count Frontenac and New France under Louis XIV.*

——, *The Old Régime in Canada.*

PEPPER, M. S., *Maids and Matrons of New France.*

WEIR, R. S., *Administration of the Old Régime in Canada.*

WOOD, W. C., *In the Heart of Old Canada.*

Living History Library

The *Living History Library* is a collection of works for children published by Bethlehem Books, comprising quality reprints of historical fiction and non-fiction, including biography. These books are chosen for their craftsmanship and for the intelligent insight they provide into the present, in light of events and personalities of the past.